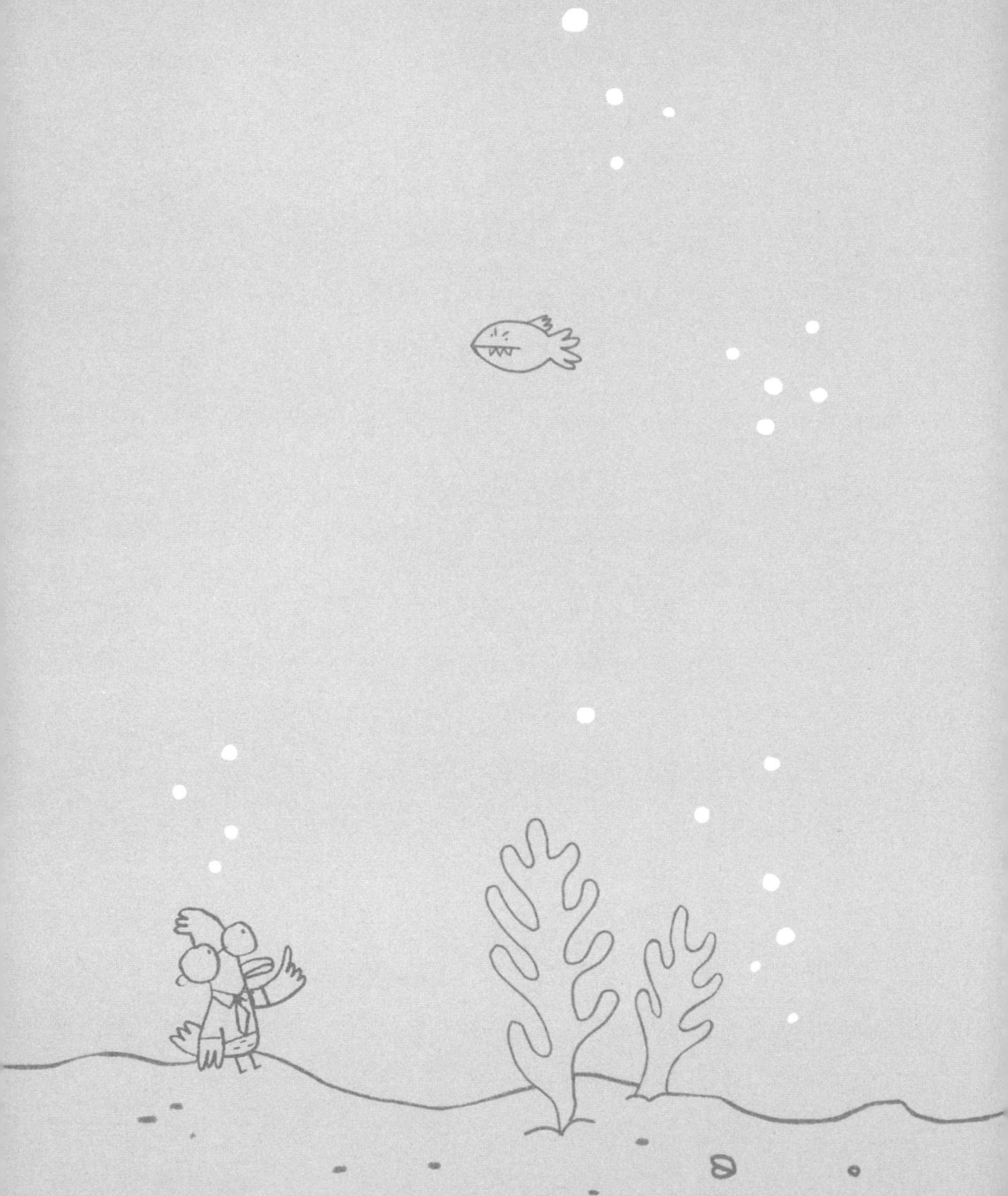

DOODLE ADVENTURES™

THE PURSUIT OF THE

PESKY PIZZA PIRATE!

DOODLE ADVENTURES™

THE PURSUIT OF THE PESKY PIZZA PIRATE!

MIKE LOWERY

WORKMAN PUBLISHING
NEW YORK

Library of Congress Cataloging-in-Publication Data is available.

ISBN 978-0-7611-8720-2

Workman books are available at special discounts when purchased in bulk for premiums and sales promotions as well as for fund-raising or educational use. Special editions or book excerpts can also be created to specification. For details, contact the Special Sales Director at the address below, or send an email to specialmarkets@workman.com.

Workman Publishing Co., Inc.
225 Varick Street
New York, NY 10014-4381
workman.com

WORKMAN is a registered trademark of Workman Publishing Co., Inc.
DOODLE ADVENTURES is a trademark of Workman Publishing Co., Inc.

Printed in China
First printing August 2016

10 9 8 7 6 5 4 3 2 1

FOR KATRIN AND ALLISTER,
MY FAVORITE PEOPLE.

THE BOOK THAT YOU'RE HOLDING IN YOUR HANDS RIGHT THIS SECOND IS DIFFERENT FROM OTHER BOOKS YOU'VE EVER HELD BEFORE.

YOU KNOW HOW YOUR PARENTS AND TEACHERS ARE ALWAYS SAYING **NOT** TO WRITE IN YOUR BOOKS??

DON'T DO IT!

WELL...

YOU'VE <u>GOT</u> TO WRITE IN THIS ONE. IT'S REQUIRED. ABSOLUTELY NECESSARY.

LET'S START NOW.
DRAW A DANCING
ROBOT HERE.
(DRAW iT QUICK! WE HAVE TO
HURRY.)

SEE, THAT WASN'T SO BAD, WAS IT?

THAT WAS OKAY, I
GUESS, BUT CAN YOU
DRAW SOMETHING
REALLY HARD?

DRAW AN UNUSUAL SUPERHERO:

OKAY. THAT WAS ACTUALLY PRETTY AWESOME.

WHO AM I?

I'M CARL.

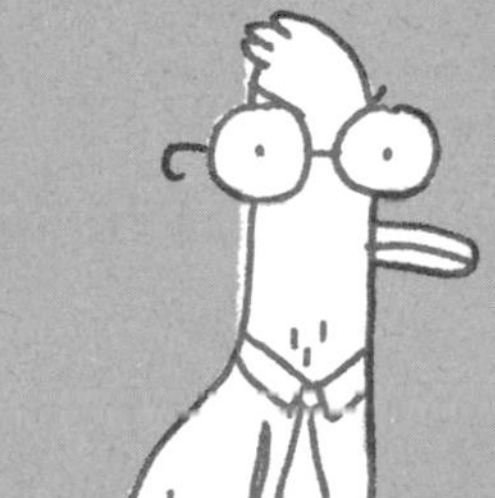

CARL THE DUCK.

HAVEN'T WE MET BEFORE?

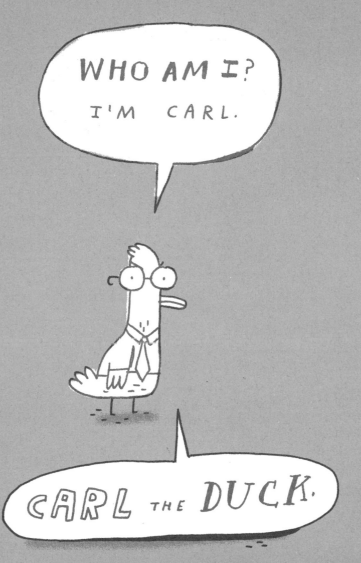

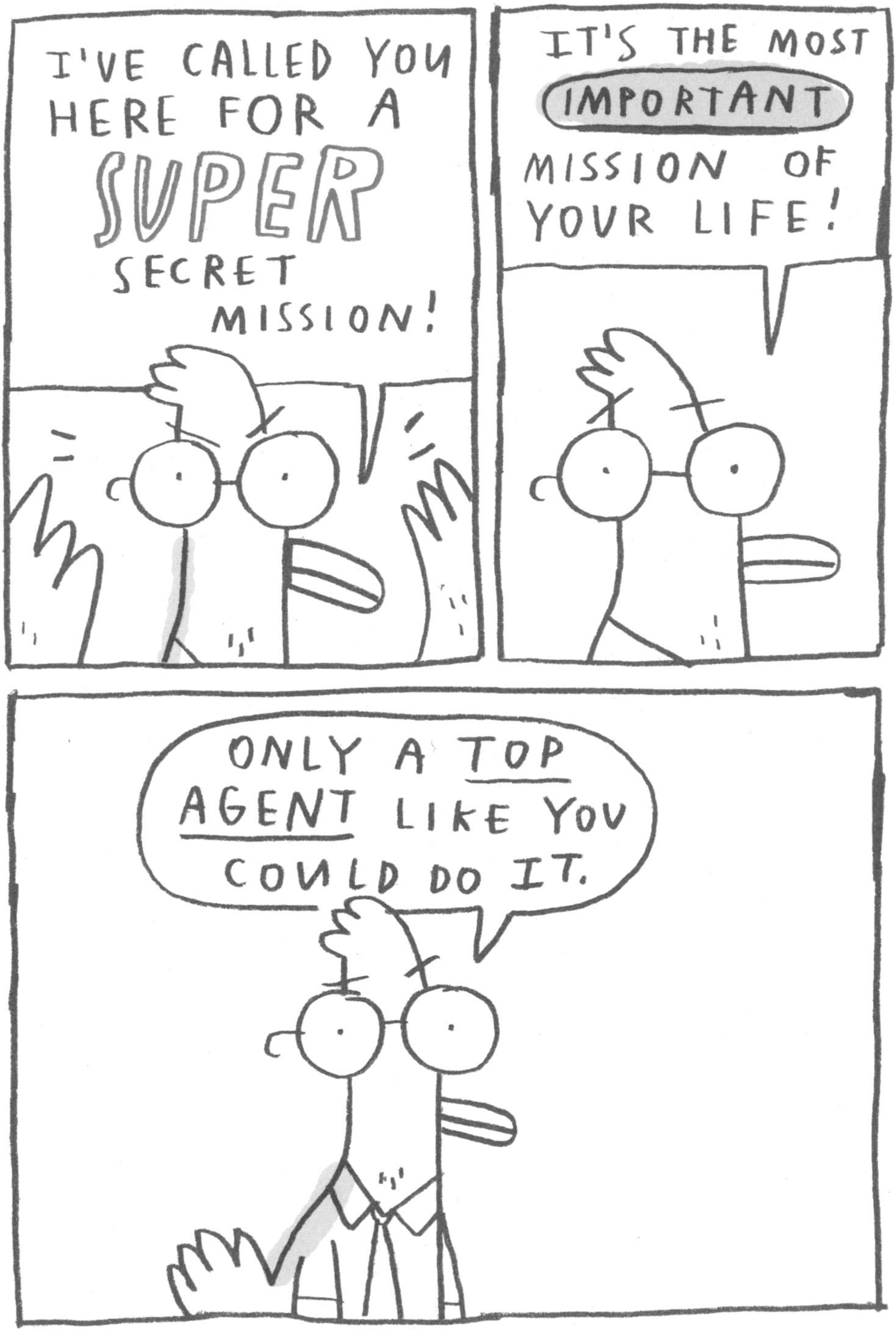
I'VE CALLED YOU HERE FOR A SUPER SECRET MISSION!
IT'S THE MOST IMPORTANT MISSION OF YOUR LIFE!
ONLY A TOP AGENT LIKE YOU COULD DO IT.

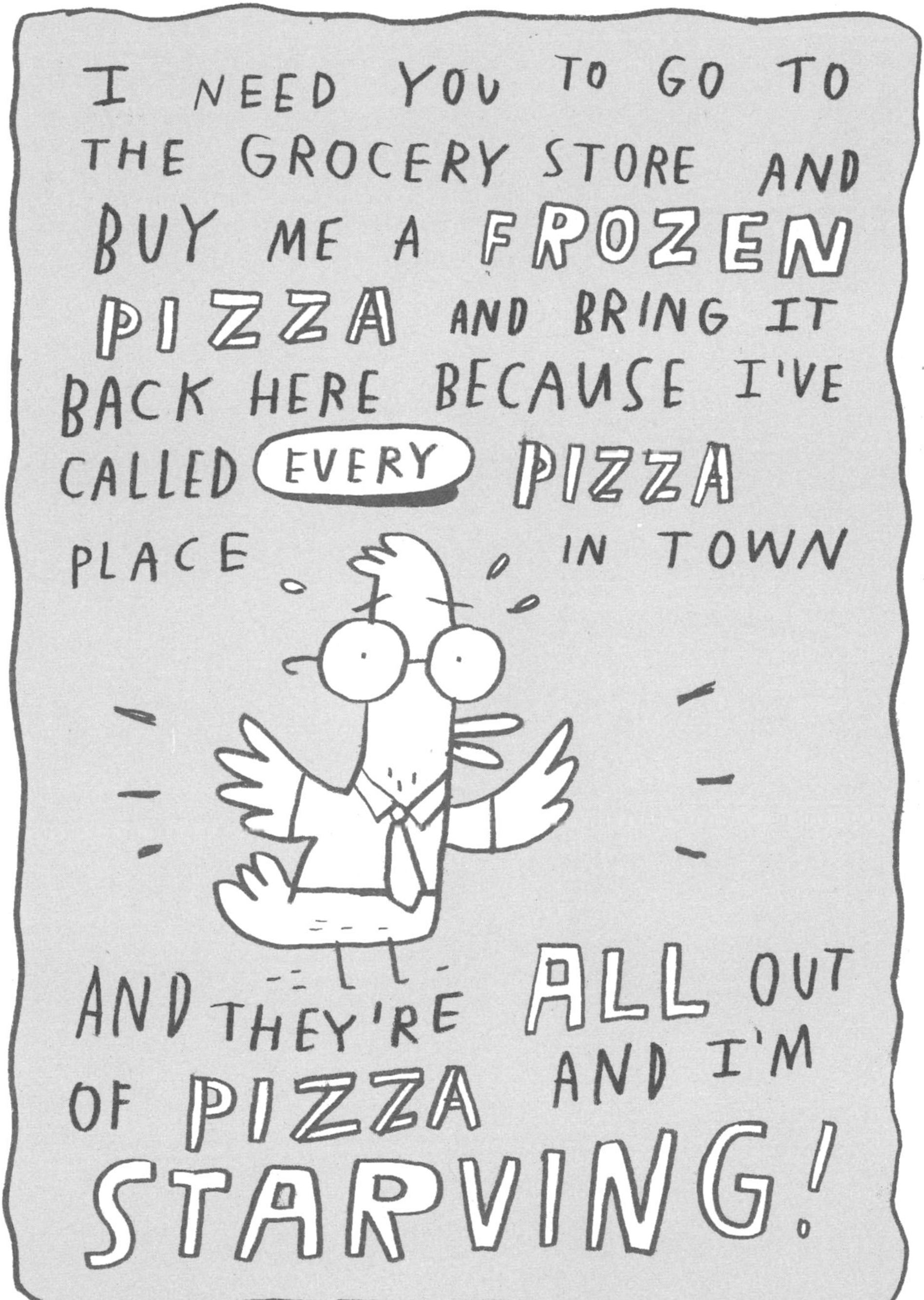
I NEED YOU TO GO TO THE GROCERY STORE AND BUY ME A FROZEN PIZZA AND BRING IT BACK HERE BECAUSE I'VE CALLED EVERY PIZZA PLACE IN TOWN AND THEY'RE ALL OUT OF PIZZA AND I'M STARVING!

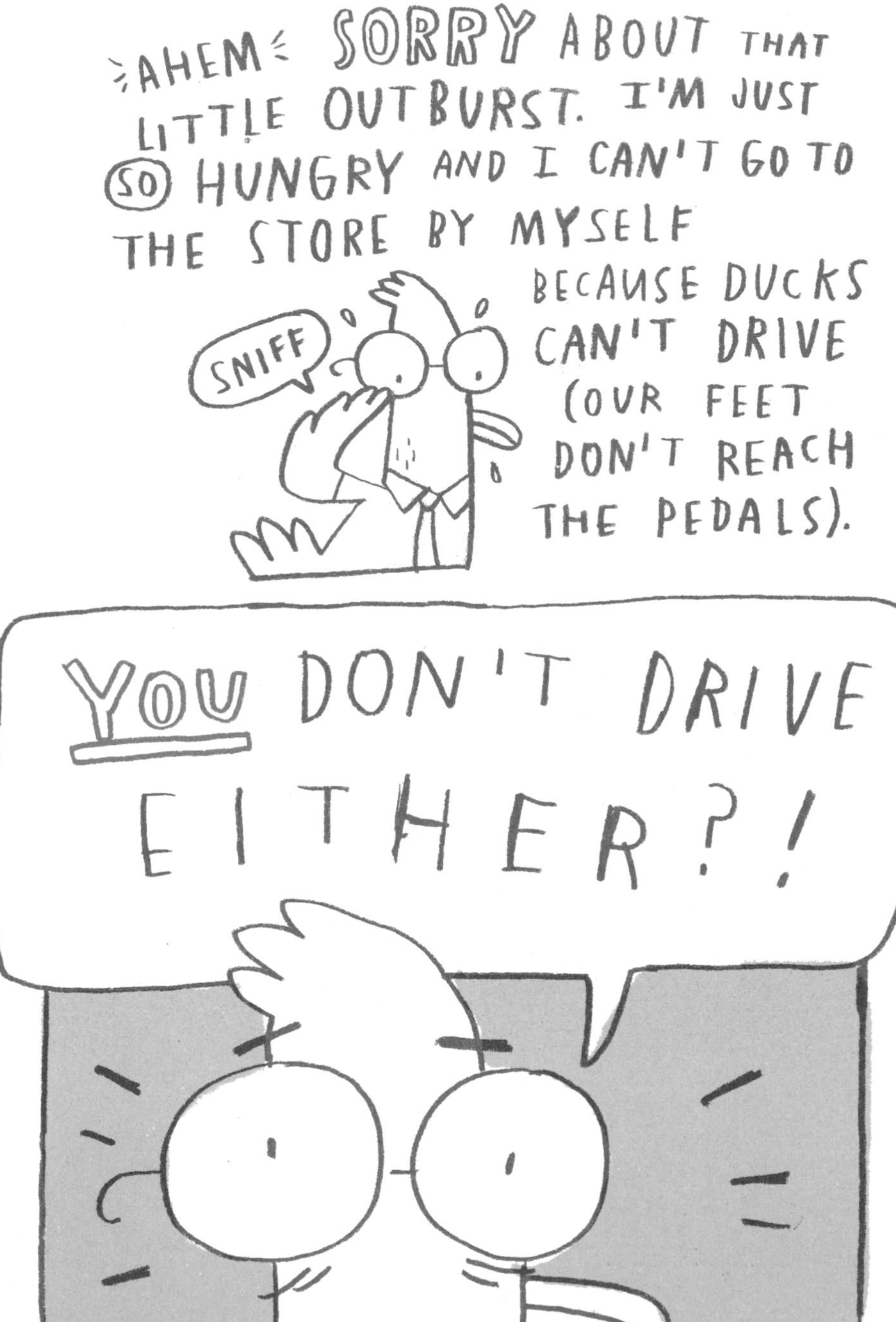
AHEM SORRY ABOUT THAT LITTLE OUTBURST. I'M JUST SO HUNGRY AND I CAN'T GO TO THE STORE BY MYSELF
SNIFF
BECAUSE DUCKS CAN'T DRIVE (OUR FEET DON'T REACH THE PEDALS).
YOU DON'T DRIVE EITHER?!

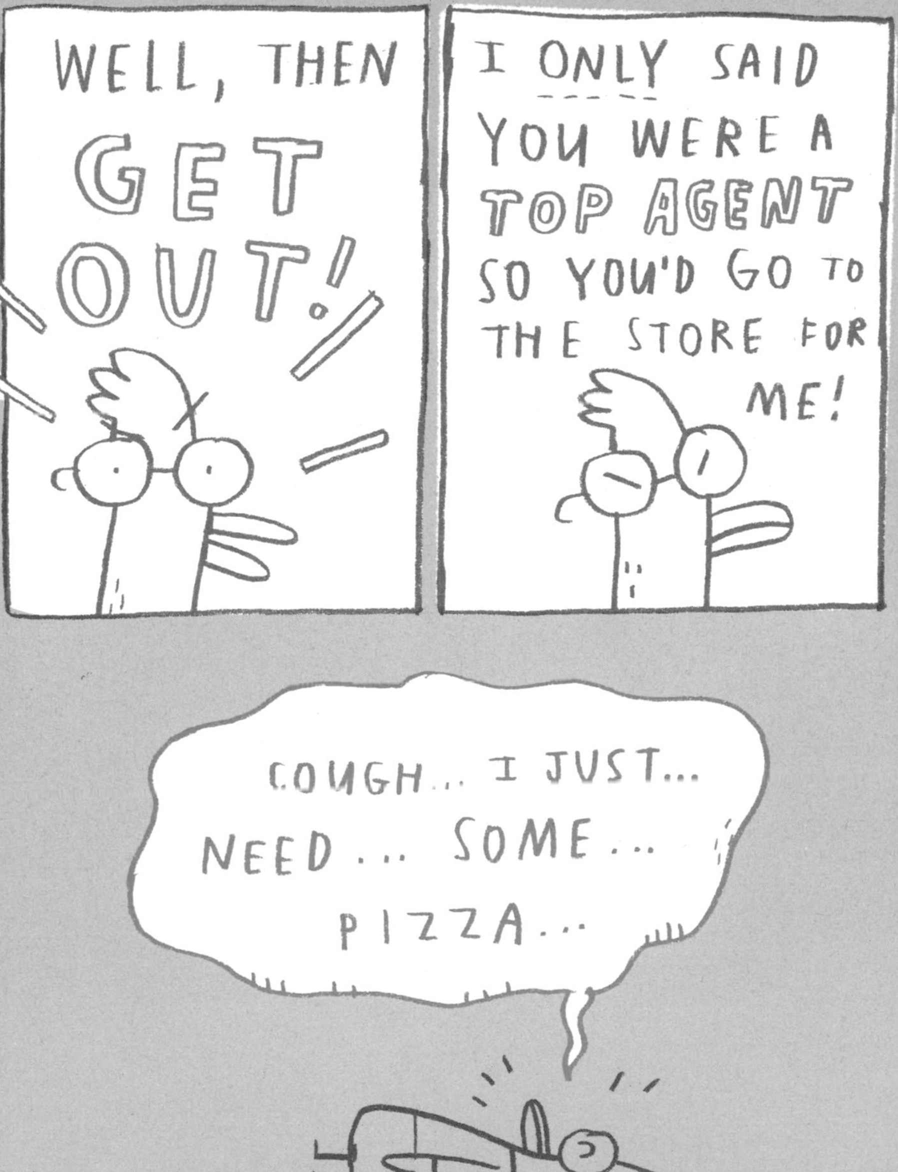
WELL, THEN GET OUT!
I ONLY SAID YOU WERE A TOP AGENT SO YOU'D GO TO THE STORE FOR ME!
COUGH... I JUST... NEED... SOME... PIZZA...

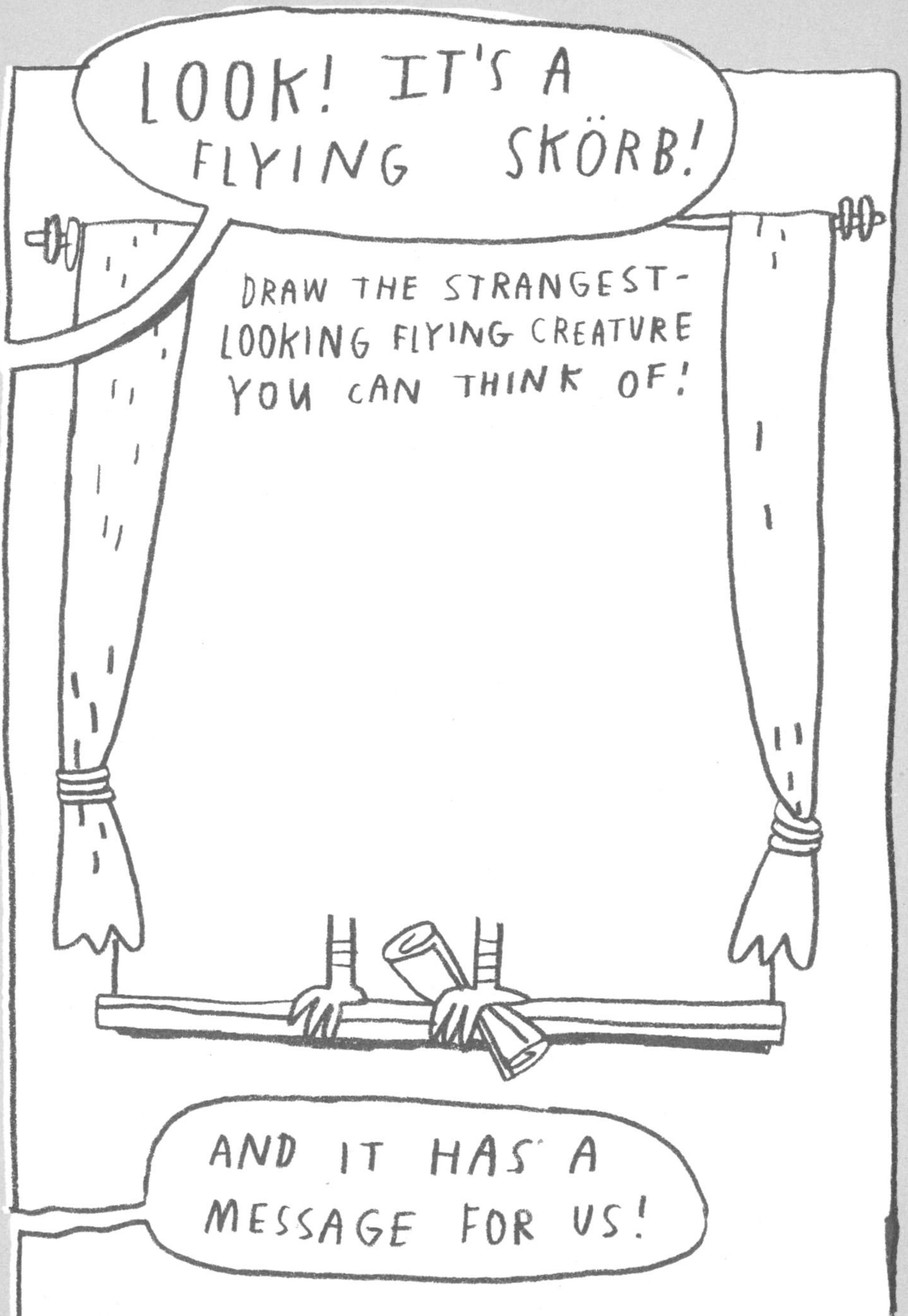
LOOK! IT'S A FLYING SKÖRB!
DRAW THE STRANGEST-LOOKING FLYING CREATURE YOU CAN THINK OF!
AND IT HAS A MESSAGE FOR US!

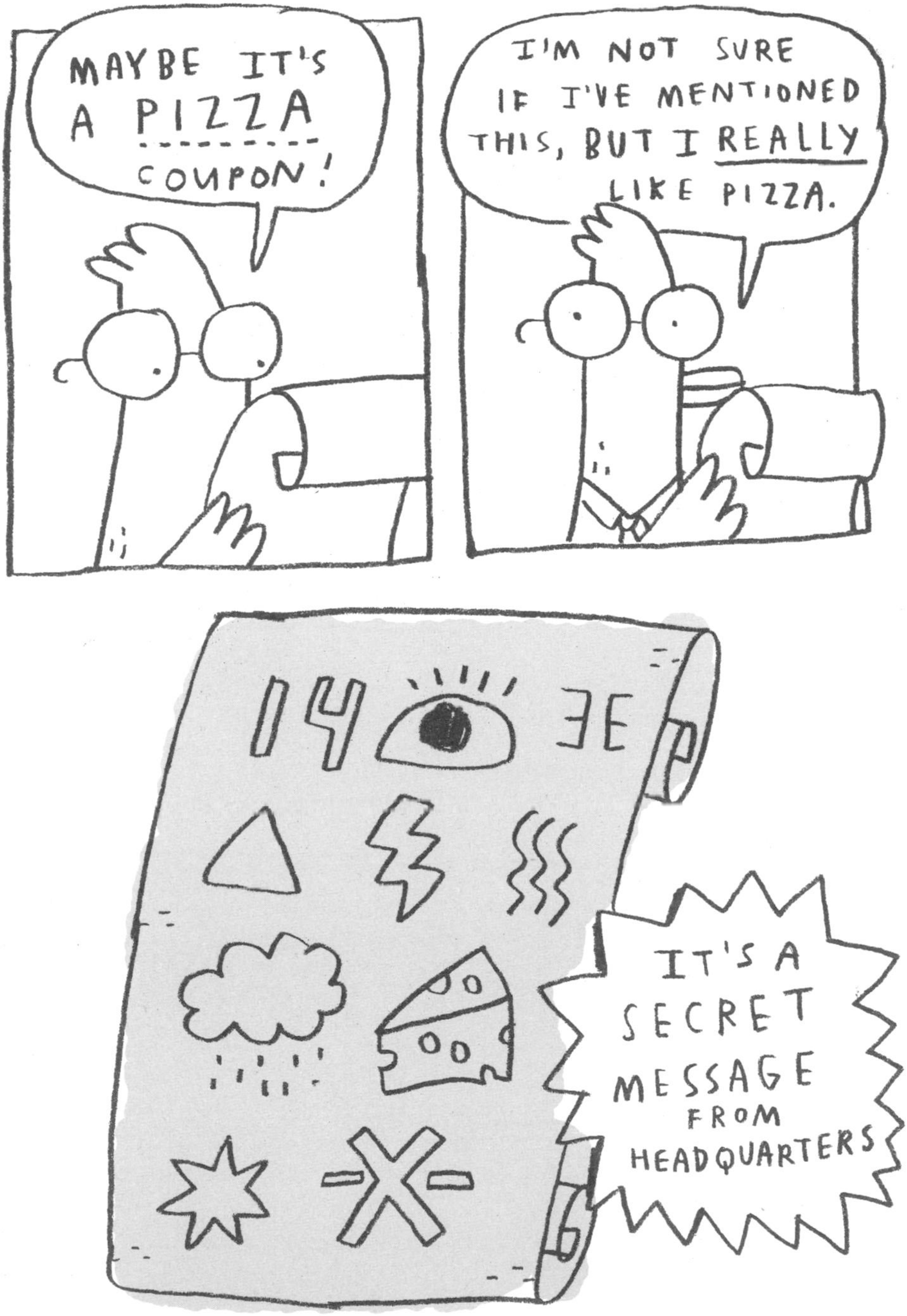
MAYBE IT'S A PIZZA COUPON!
I'M NOT SURE IF I'VE MENTIONED THIS, BUT I REALLY LIKE PIZZA.
IT'S A SECRET MESSAGE FROM HEADQUARTERS

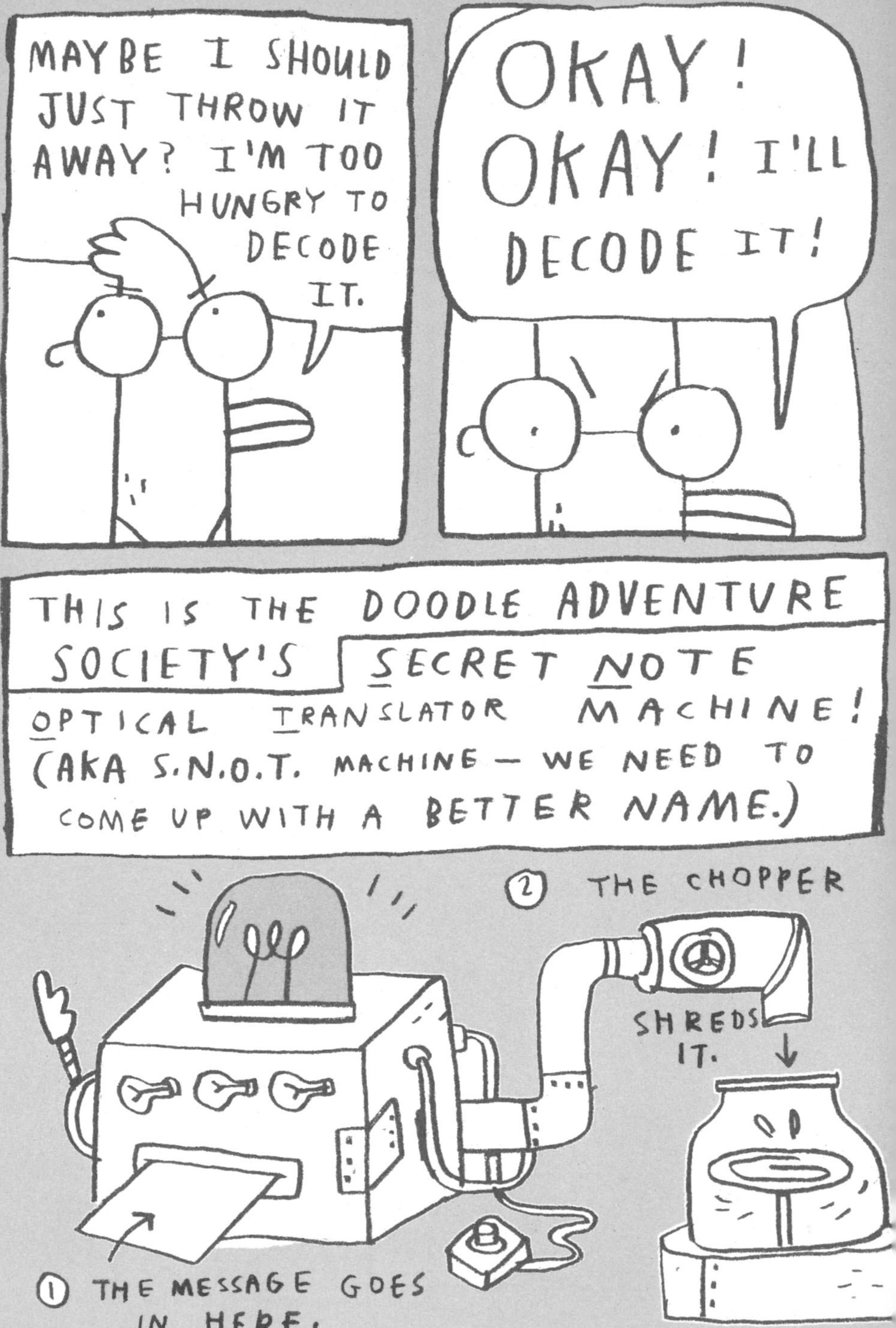
MAYBE I SHOULD JUST THROW IT AWAY? I'M TOO HUNGRY TO DECODE IT.
OKAY! OKAY! I'LL DECODE IT!
THIS IS THE DOODLE ADVENTURE SOCIETY'S SECRET NOTE OPTICAL TRANSLATOR MACHINE! (AKA S.N.O.T. MACHINE — WE NEED TO COME UP WITH A BETTER NAME.)
② THE CHOPPER
SHREDS IT.
① THE MESSAGE GOES IN HERE.

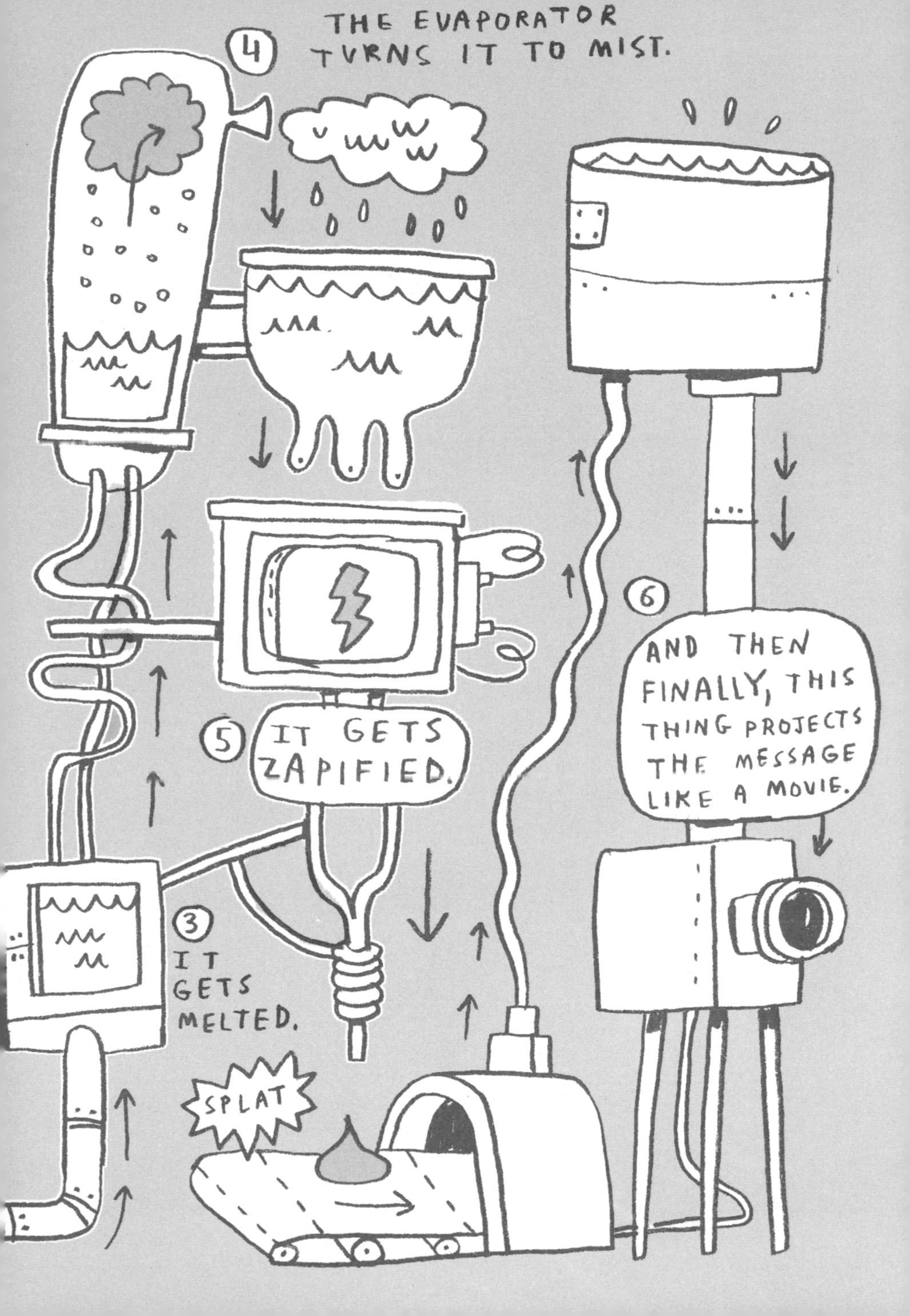
4
THE EVAPORATOR TURNS IT TO MIST.
5
IT GETS ZAPIFIED.
6
AND THEN FINALLY, THIS THING PROJECTS THE MESSAGE LIKE A MOVIE.
3
IT GETS MELTED.
SPLAT

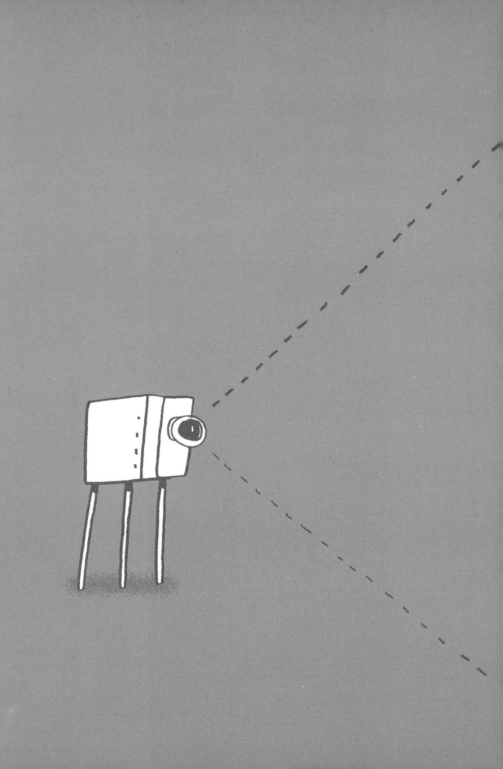

CARL, SOME AWFUL PERSON IS GOING AROUND TOWN STEALING ALL OF THE PIZZAS (AND) ALL OF THE PIZZA TOPPINGS! TAKE THE NEW RECRUIT AND

GO FIND THOSE PIZZAS !!!

o o o

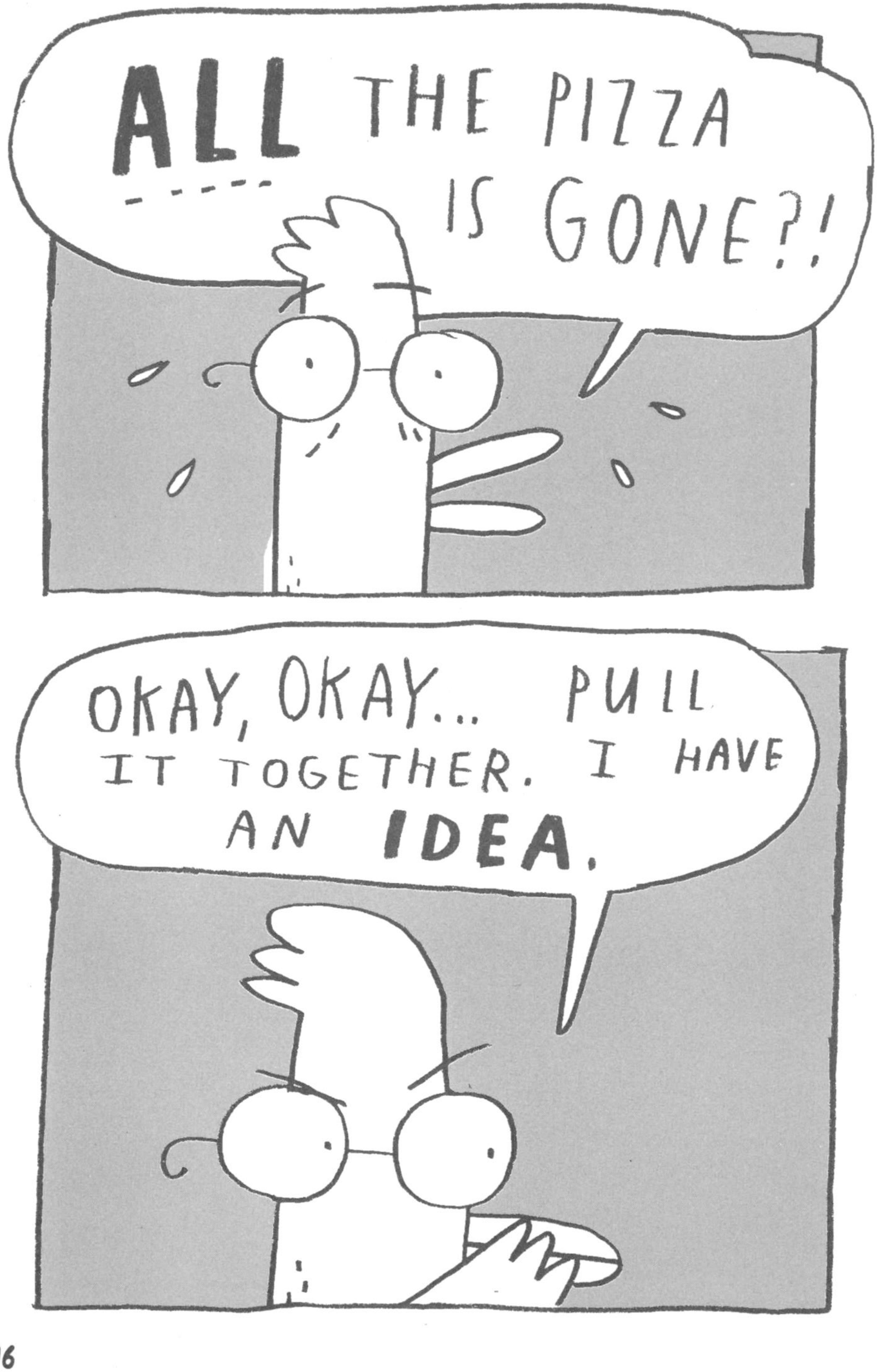
ALL THE PIZZA IS GONE?!
OKAY, OKAY... PULL IT TOGETHER. I HAVE AN IDEA.

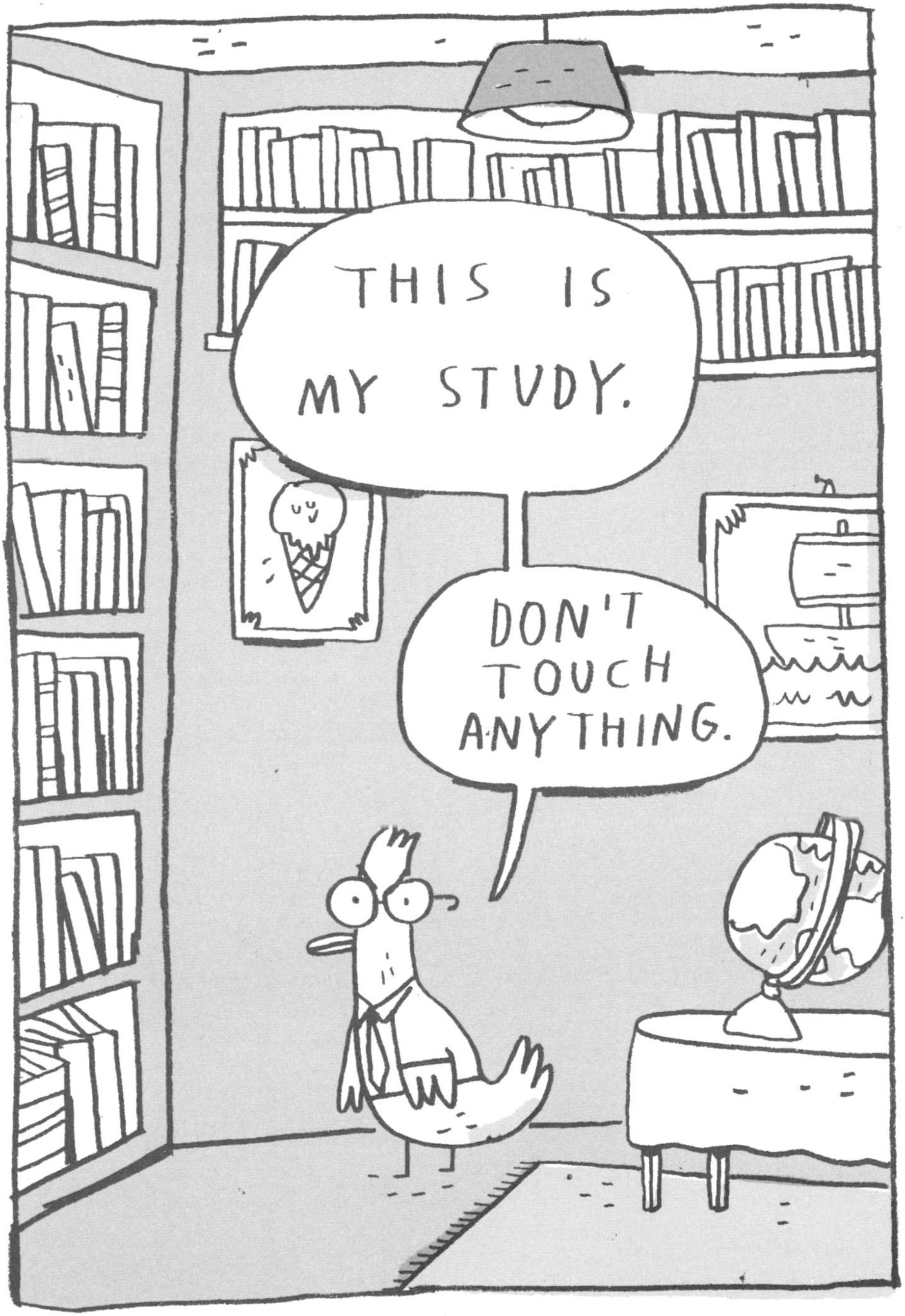
THIS IS MY STUDY.
DON'T TOUCH ANYTHING.

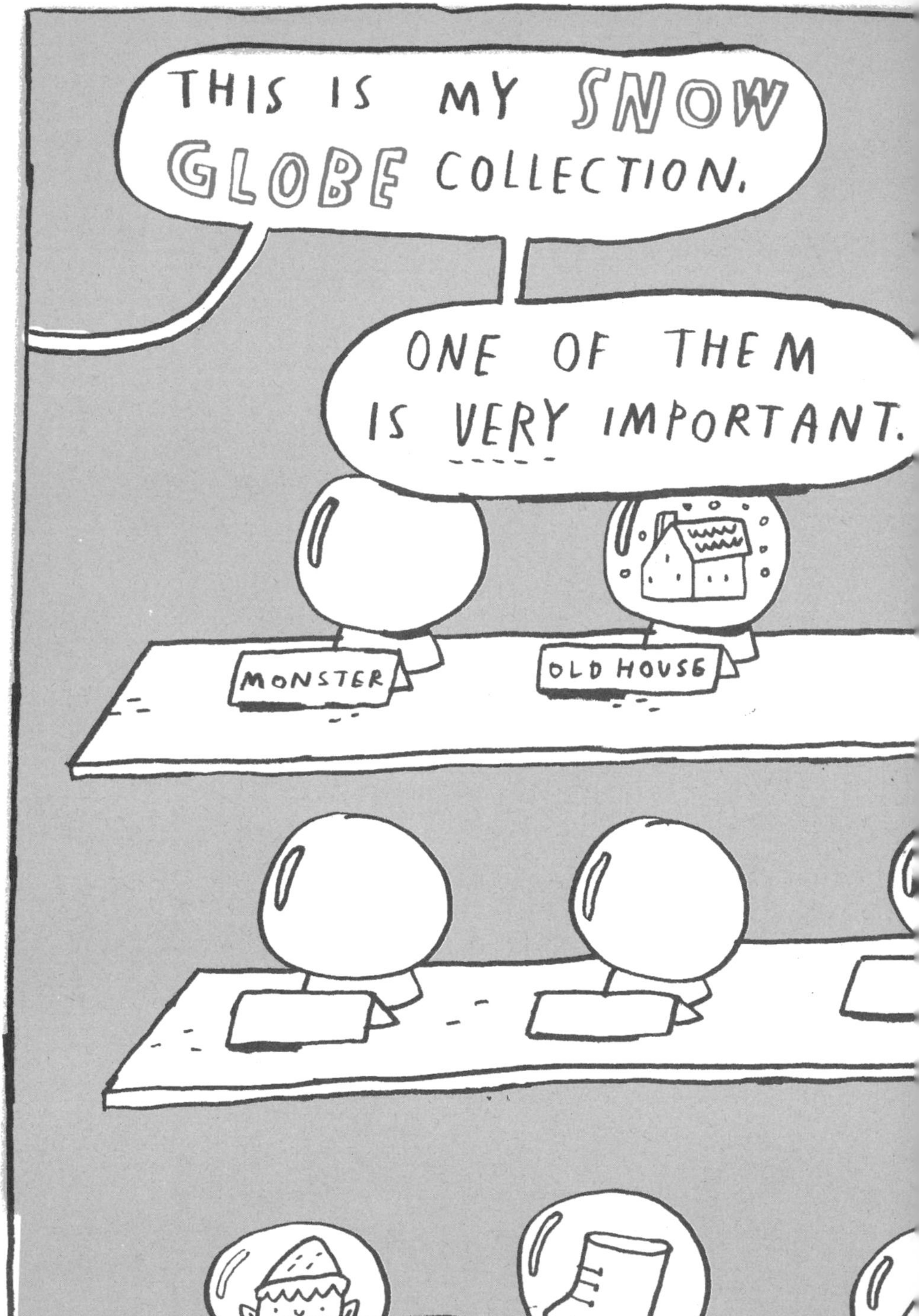
THIS IS MY SNOW GLOBE COLLECTION.
ONE OF THEM IS VERY IMPORTANT.
MONSTER
OLD HOUSE

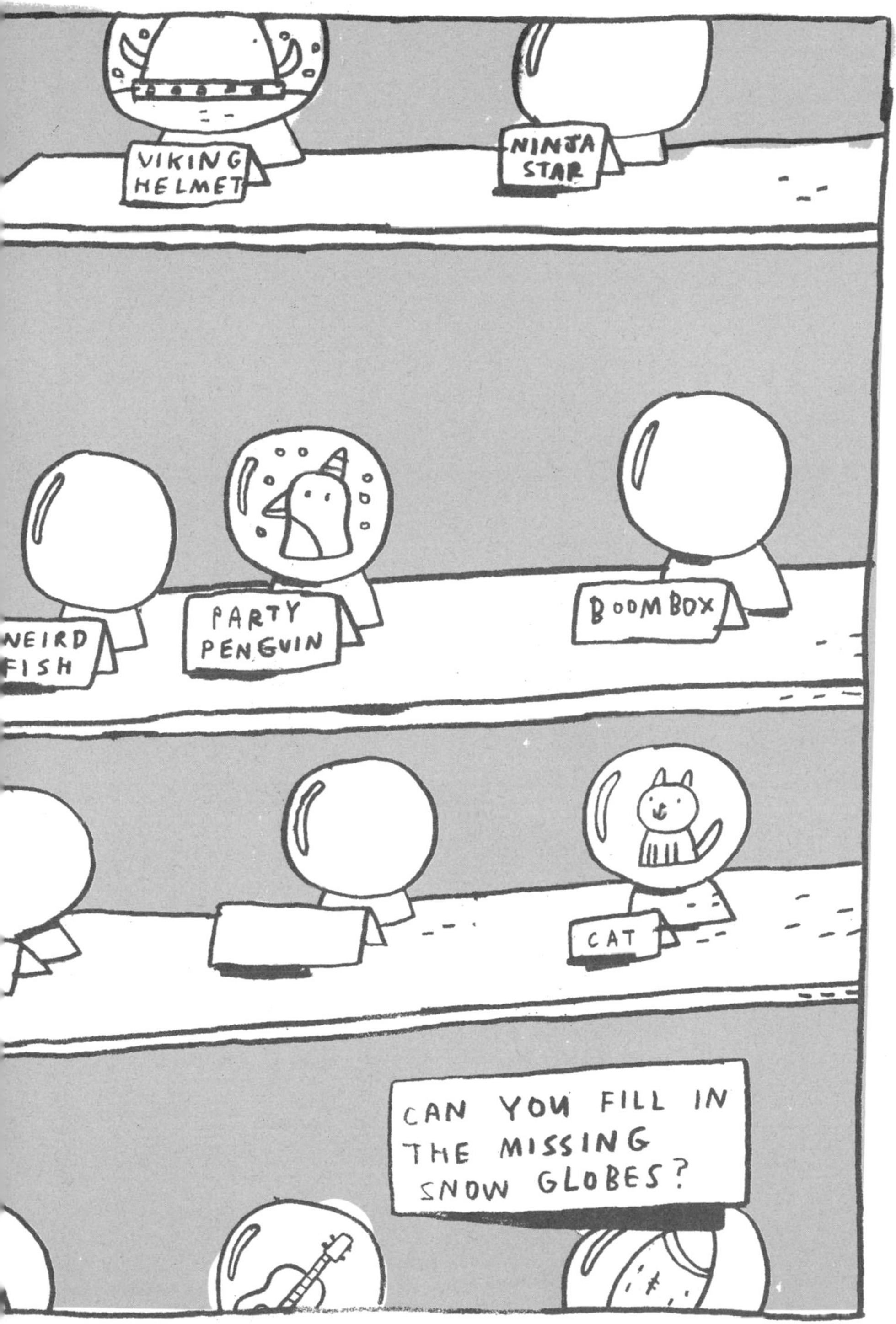
VIKING HELMET
NINJA STAR
WEIRD FISH
PARTY PENGUIN
BOOMBOX
CAT
CAN YOU FILL IN THE MISSING SNOW GLOBES?

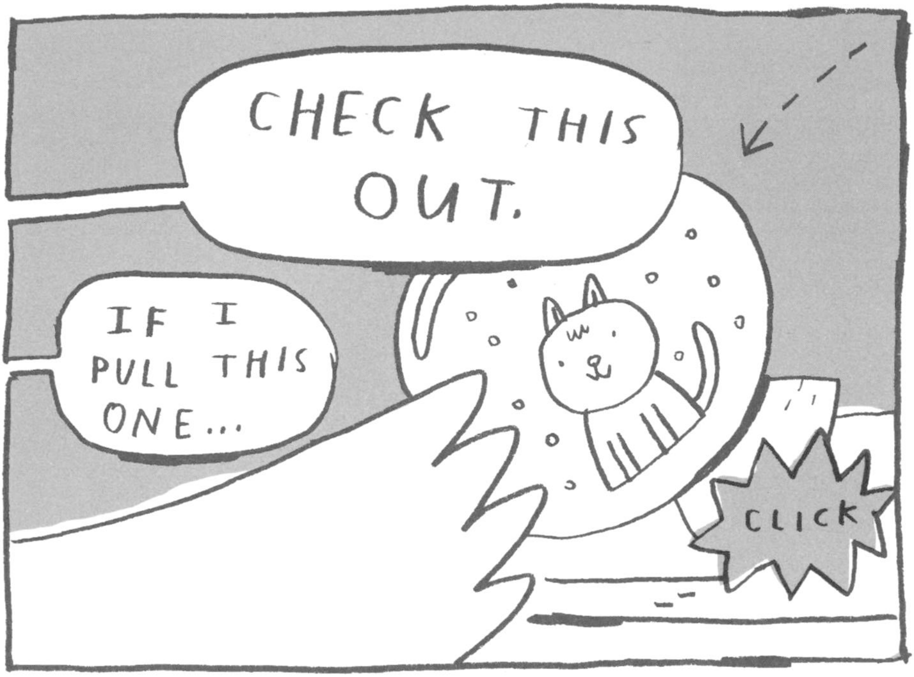
CHECK THIS OUT.
IF I PULL THIS ONE...
CLICK

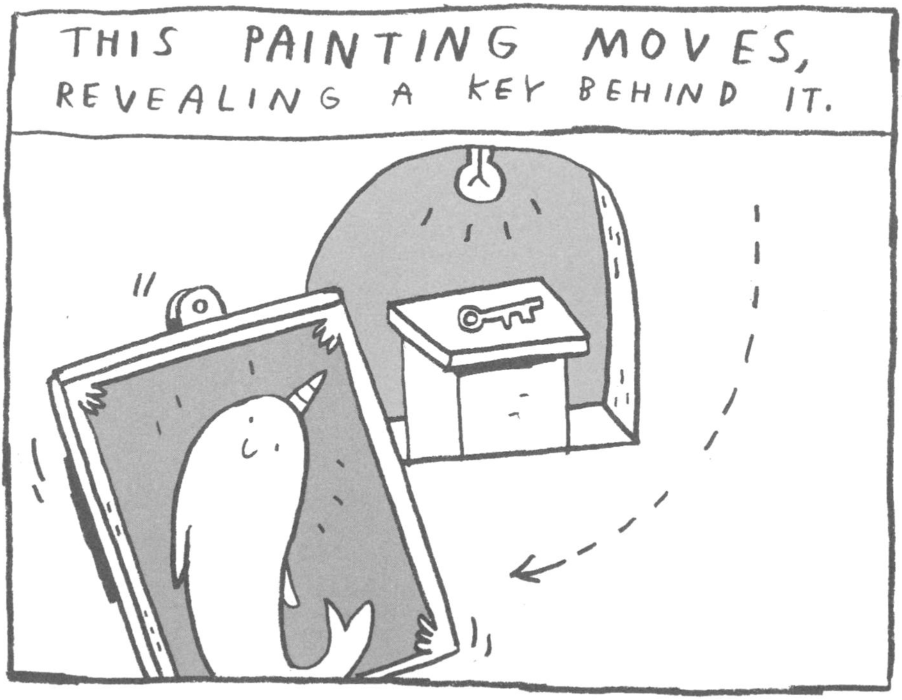
THIS PAINTING MOVES, REVEALING A KEY BEHIND IT.

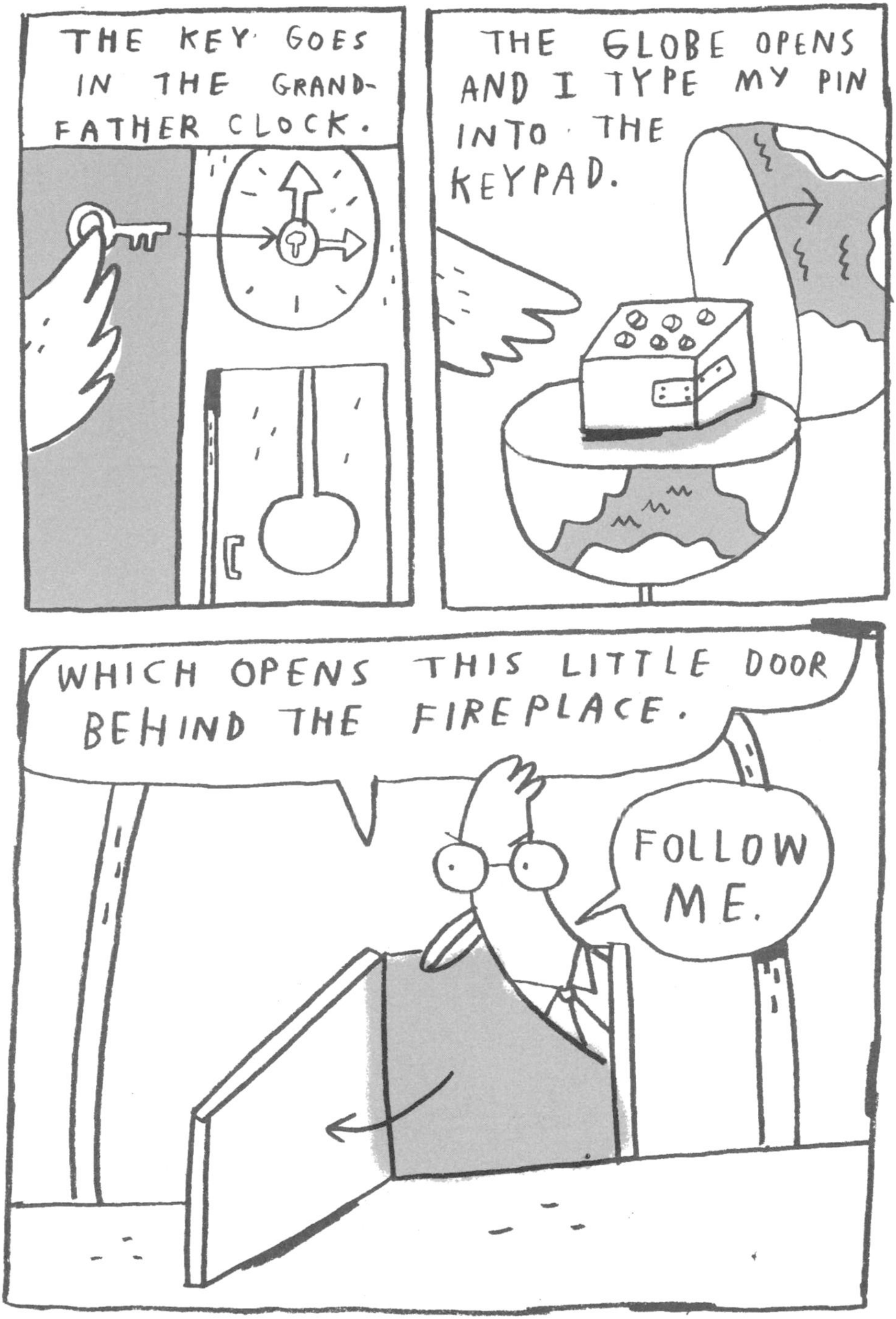
THE KEY GOES IN THE GRAND-FATHER CLOCK.
THE GLOBE OPENS AND I TYPE MY PIN INTO THE KEYPAD.
WHICH OPENS THIS LITTLE DOOR BEHIND THE FIREPLACE.
FOLLOW ME.

THIS IS THE SEARCH-A-TRON 3000 COMPUTER. LET'S USE IT TO SEARCH THE **RBGDB.**

(REALLY BAD GUY DATABASE)

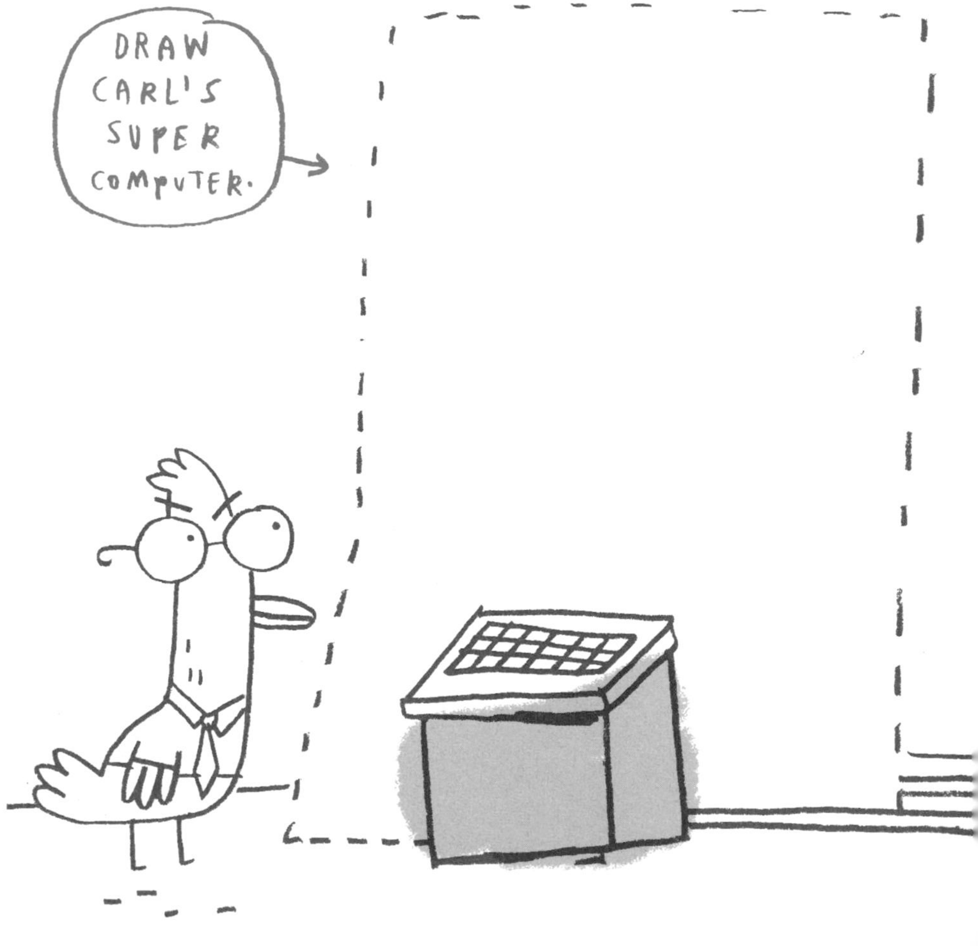
DRAW CARL'S SUPER COMPUTER.

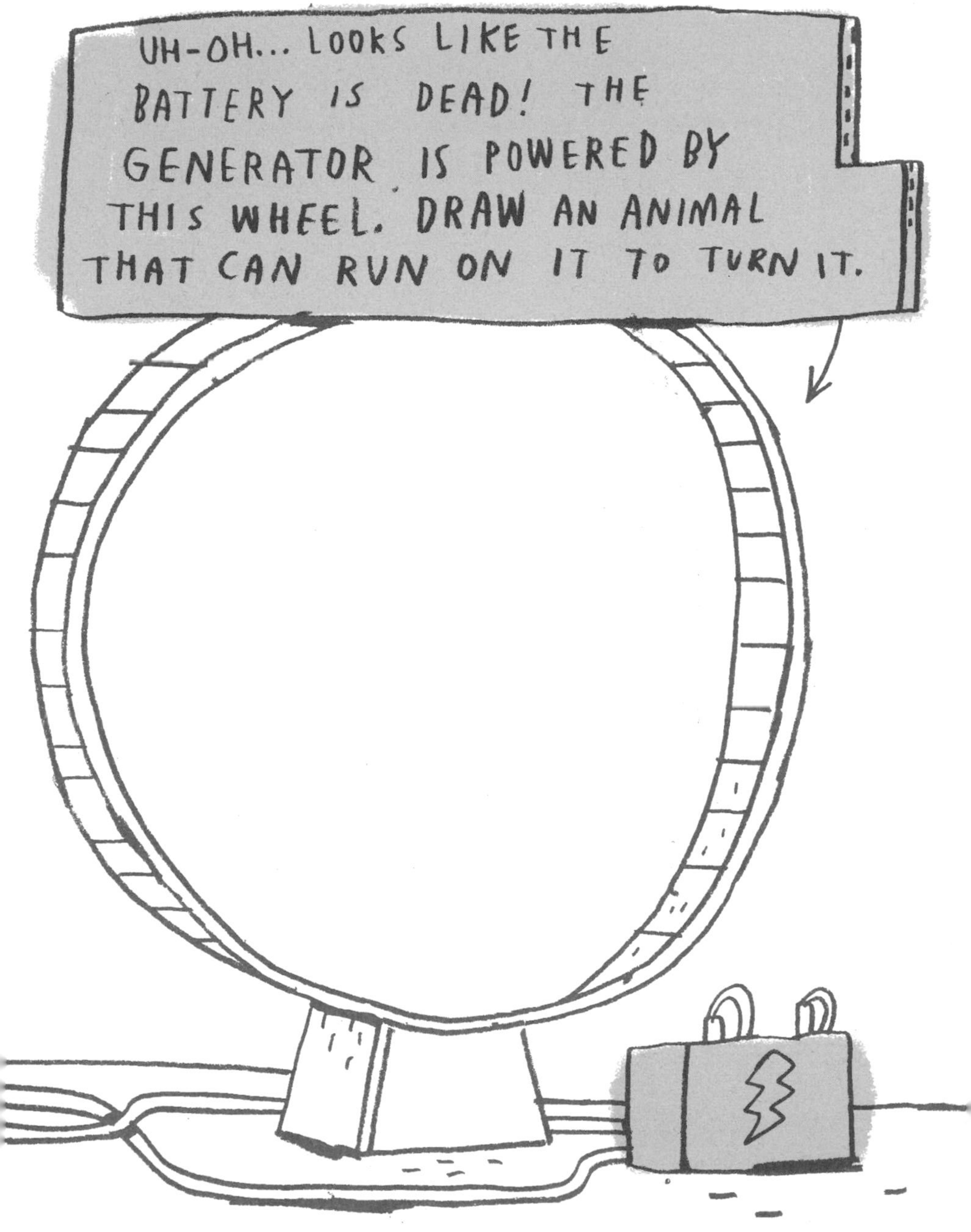
UH-OH... LOOKS LIKE THE BATTERY IS DEAD! THE GENERATOR IS POWERED BY THIS WHEEL. DRAW AN ANIMAL THAT CAN RUN ON IT TO TURN IT.

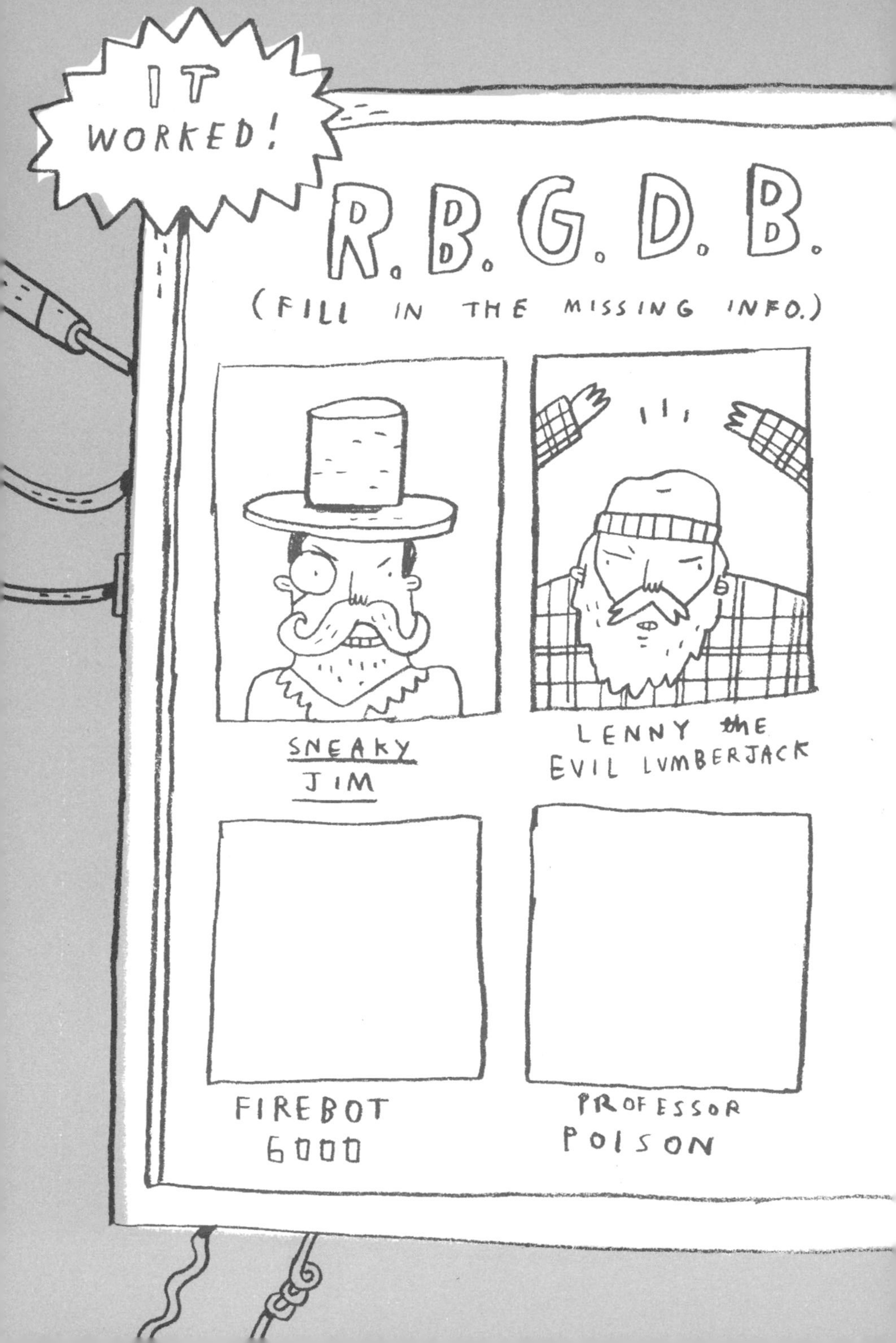
IT WORKED!
R.B.G.D.B.
(FILL IN THE MISSING INFO.)
SNEAKY JIM
LENNY the EVIL LUMBERJACK
FIREBOT 6000
PROFESSOR POISON

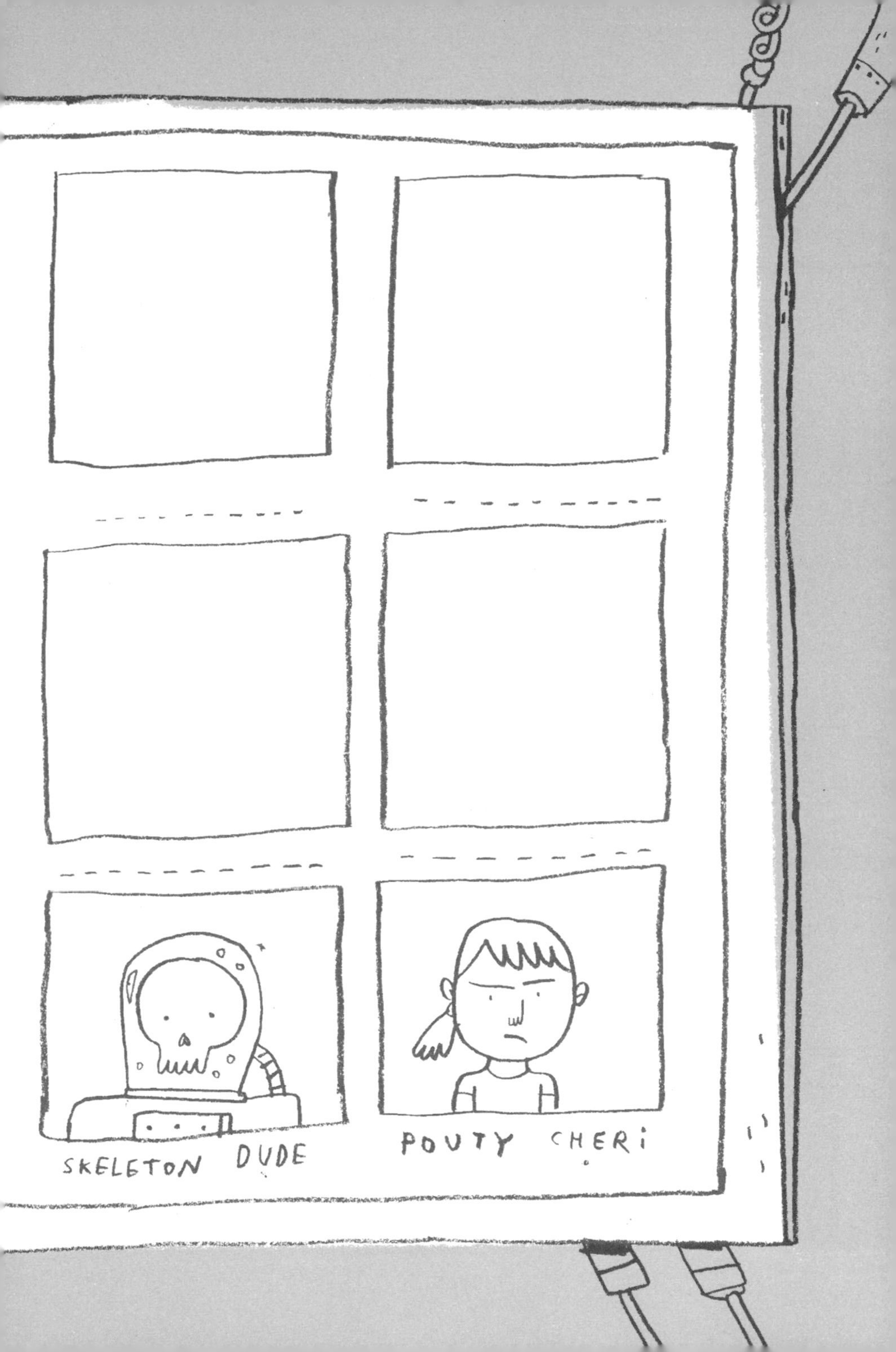
SKELETON DUDE
POUTY CHERI

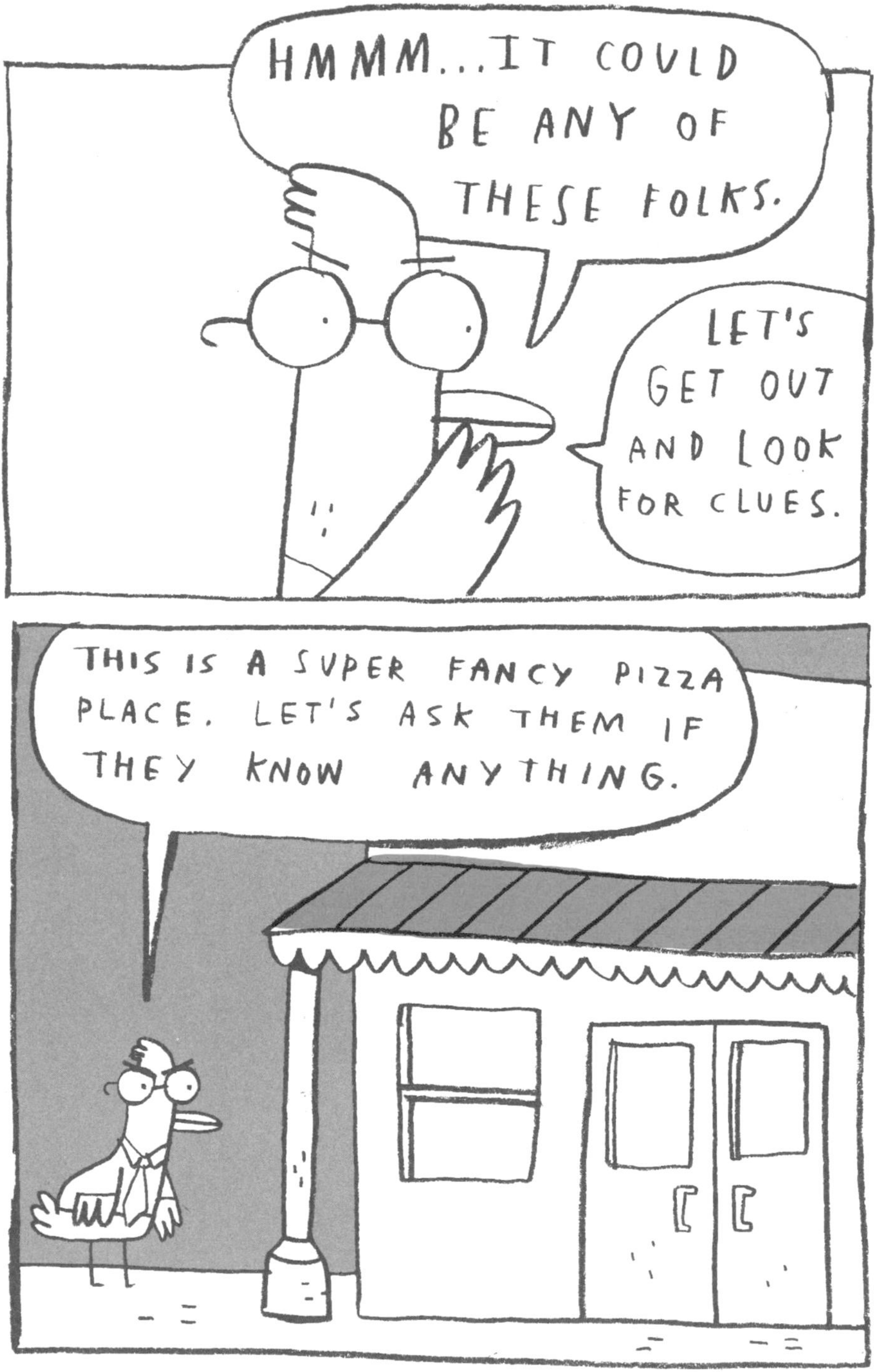
HMMM...IT COULD BE ANY OF THESE FOLKS.
LET'S GET OUT AND LOOK FOR CLUES.
THIS IS A SUPER FANCY PIZZA PLACE. LET'S ASK THEM IF THEY KNOW ANYTHING.

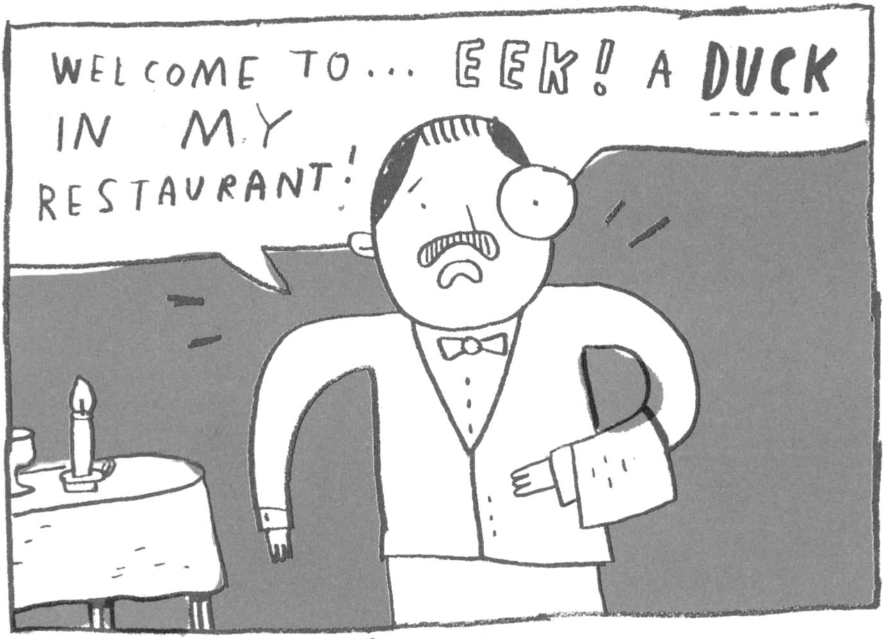
WELCOME TO... EEK! A DUCK IN MY RESTAURANT!

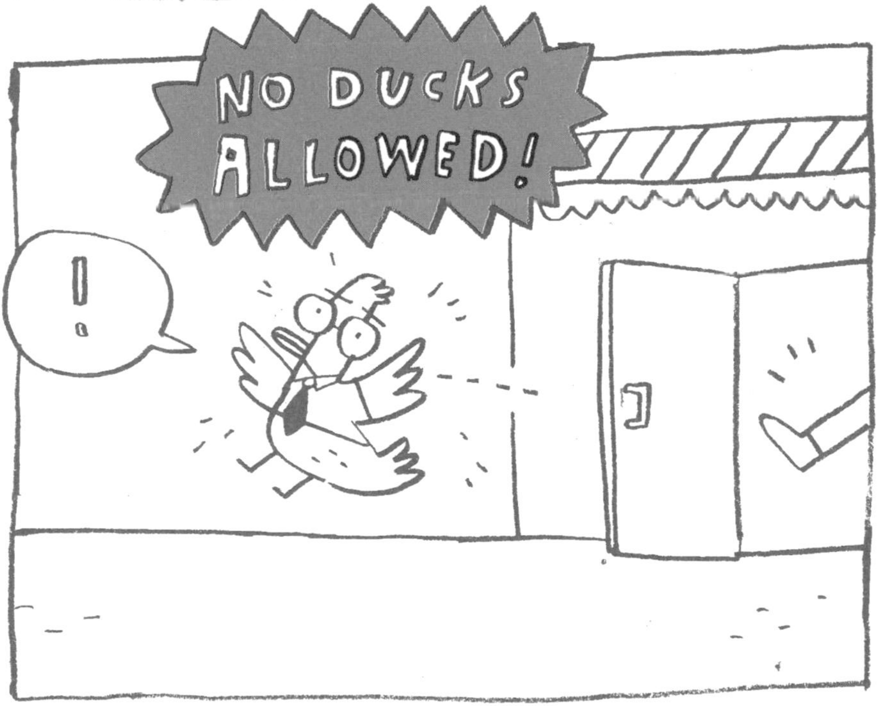
NO DUCKS ALLOWED!
!

CARL NEEDS A DISGUISE.

USE THESE ITEMS (OR MAKE UP YOUR OWN).

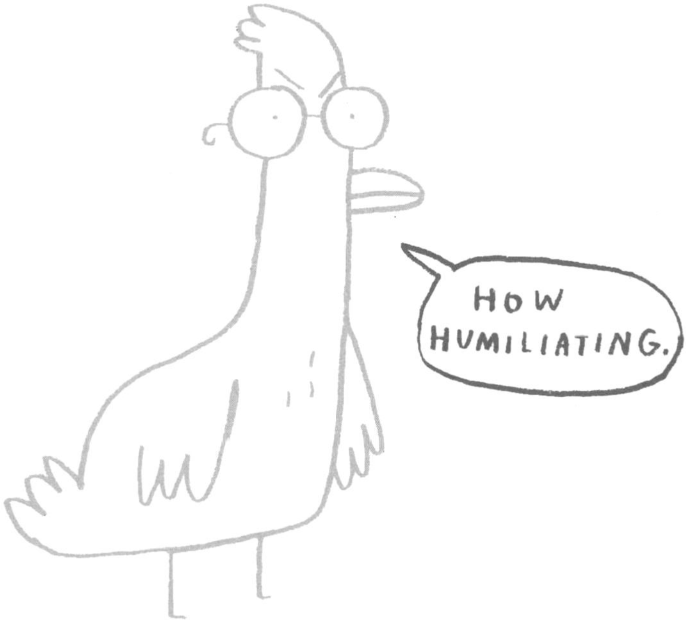
HOW HUMILIATING.

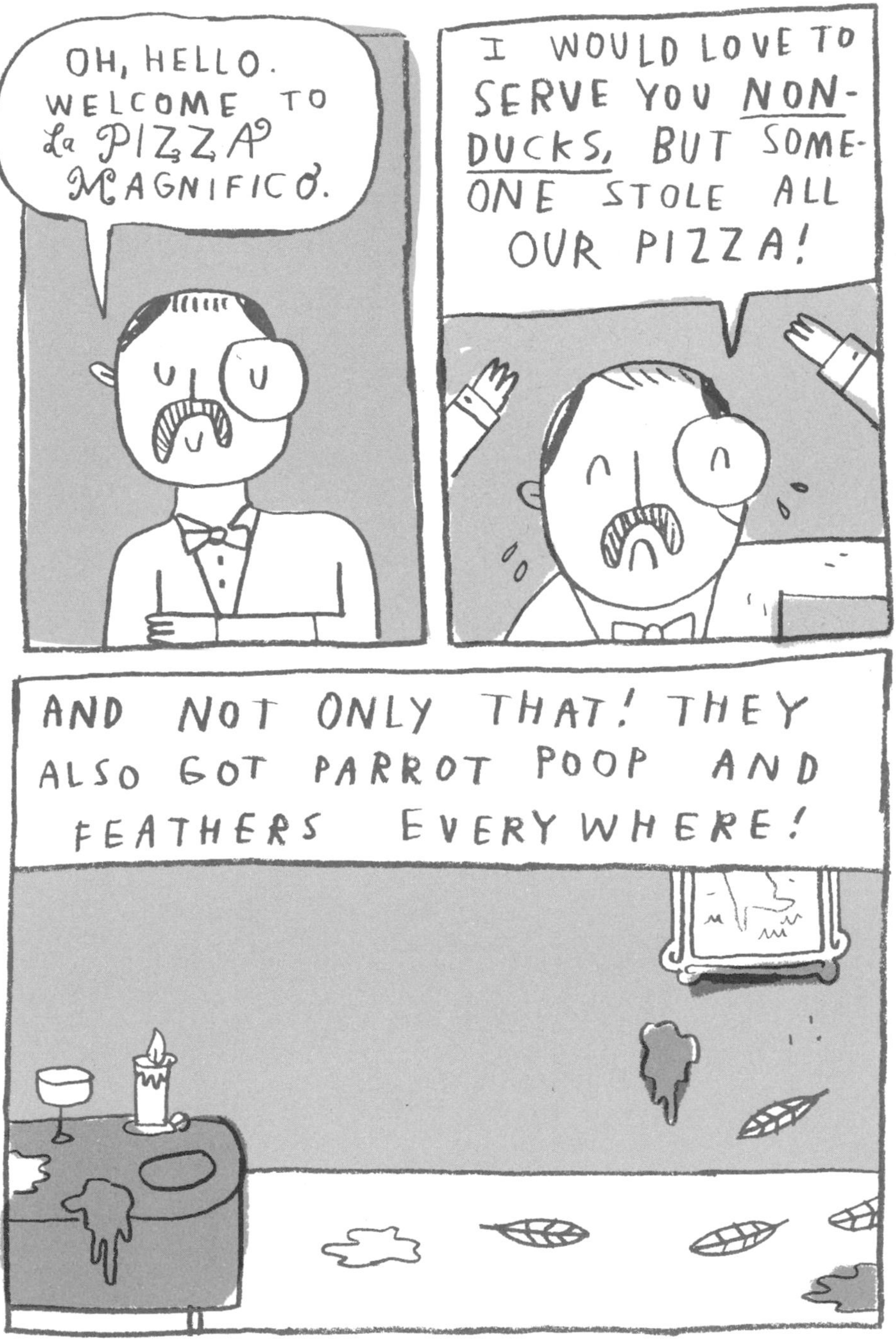
OH, HELLO. WELCOME TO La PIZZA MAGNIFICO.
I WOULD LOVE TO SERVE YOU NON-DUCKS, BUT SOMEONE STOLE ALL OUR PIZZA!
AND NOT ONLY THAT! THEY ALSO GOT PARROT POOP AND FEATHERS EVERYWHERE!

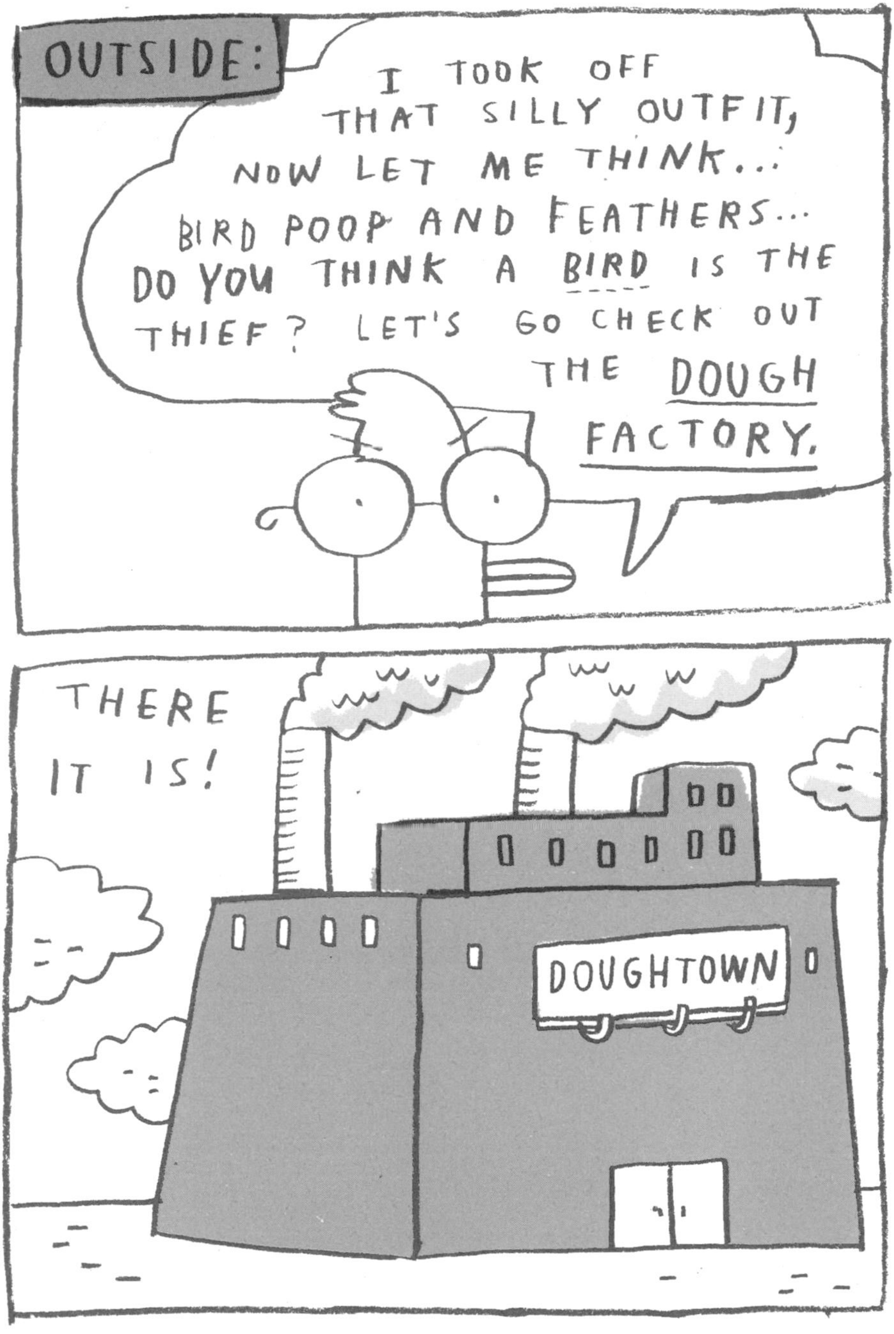
OUTSIDE:
I TOOK OFF THAT SILLY OUTFIT, NOW LET ME THINK... BIRD POOP AND FEATHERS... DO YOU THINK A BIRD IS THE THIEF? LET'S GO CHECK OUT THE DOUGH FACTORY.
THERE IT IS!
DOUGHTOWN

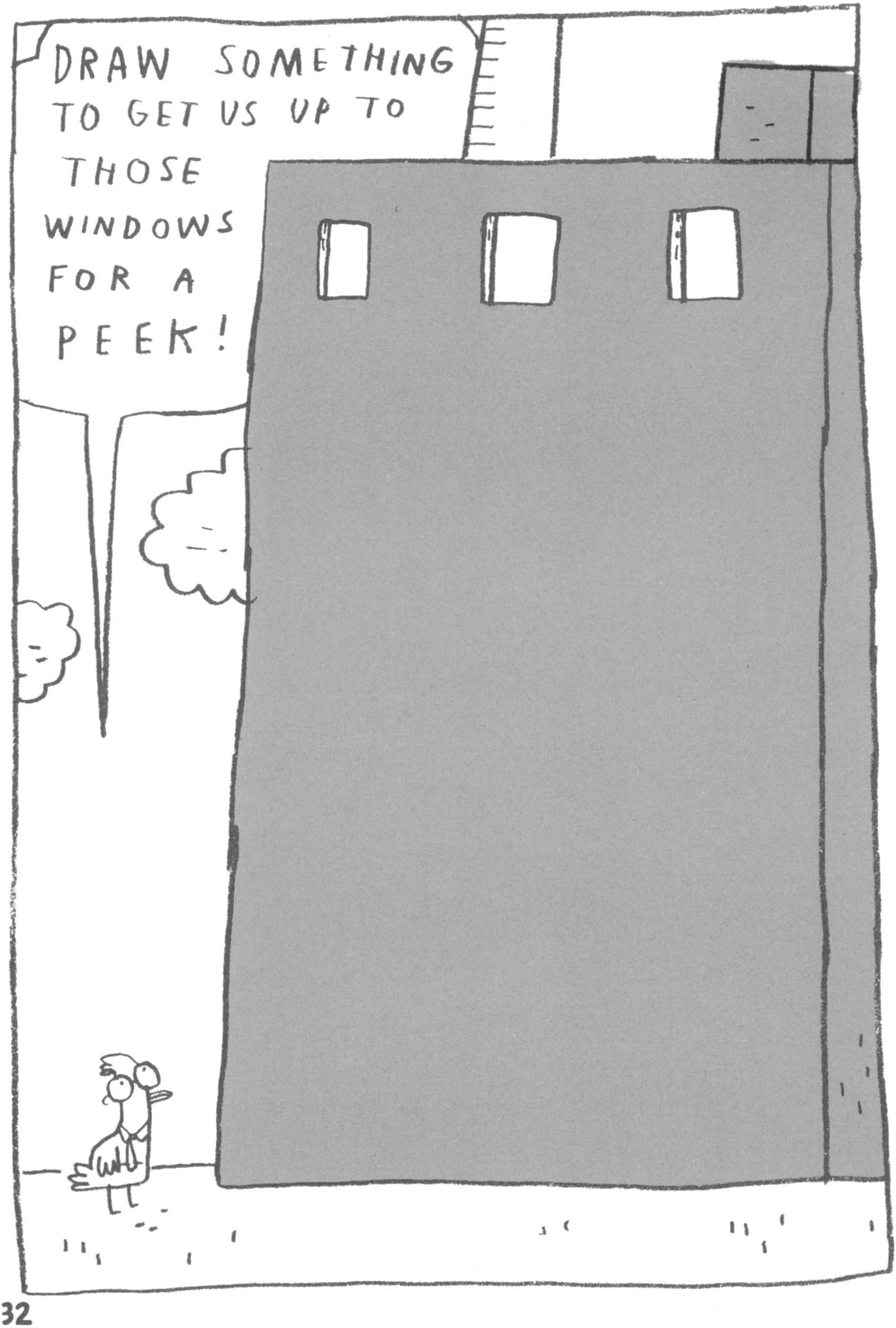
DRAW SOMETHING TO GET US UP TO THOSE WINDOWS FOR A PEEK!

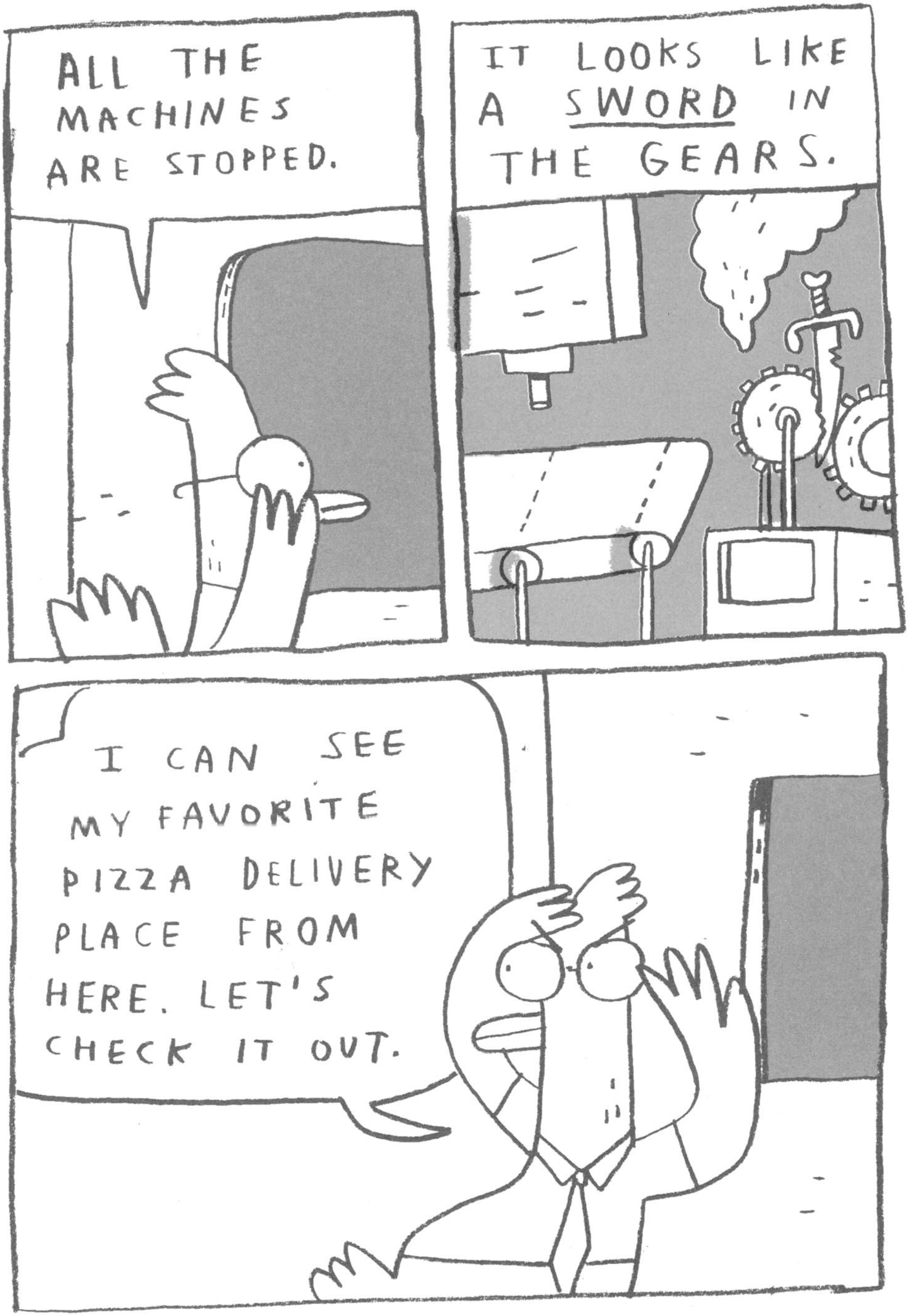
ALL THE MACHINES ARE STOPPED.
IT LOOKS LIKE A SWORD IN THE GEARS.
I CAN SEE MY FAVORITE PIZZA DELIVERY PLACE FROM HERE. LET'S CHECK IT OUT.

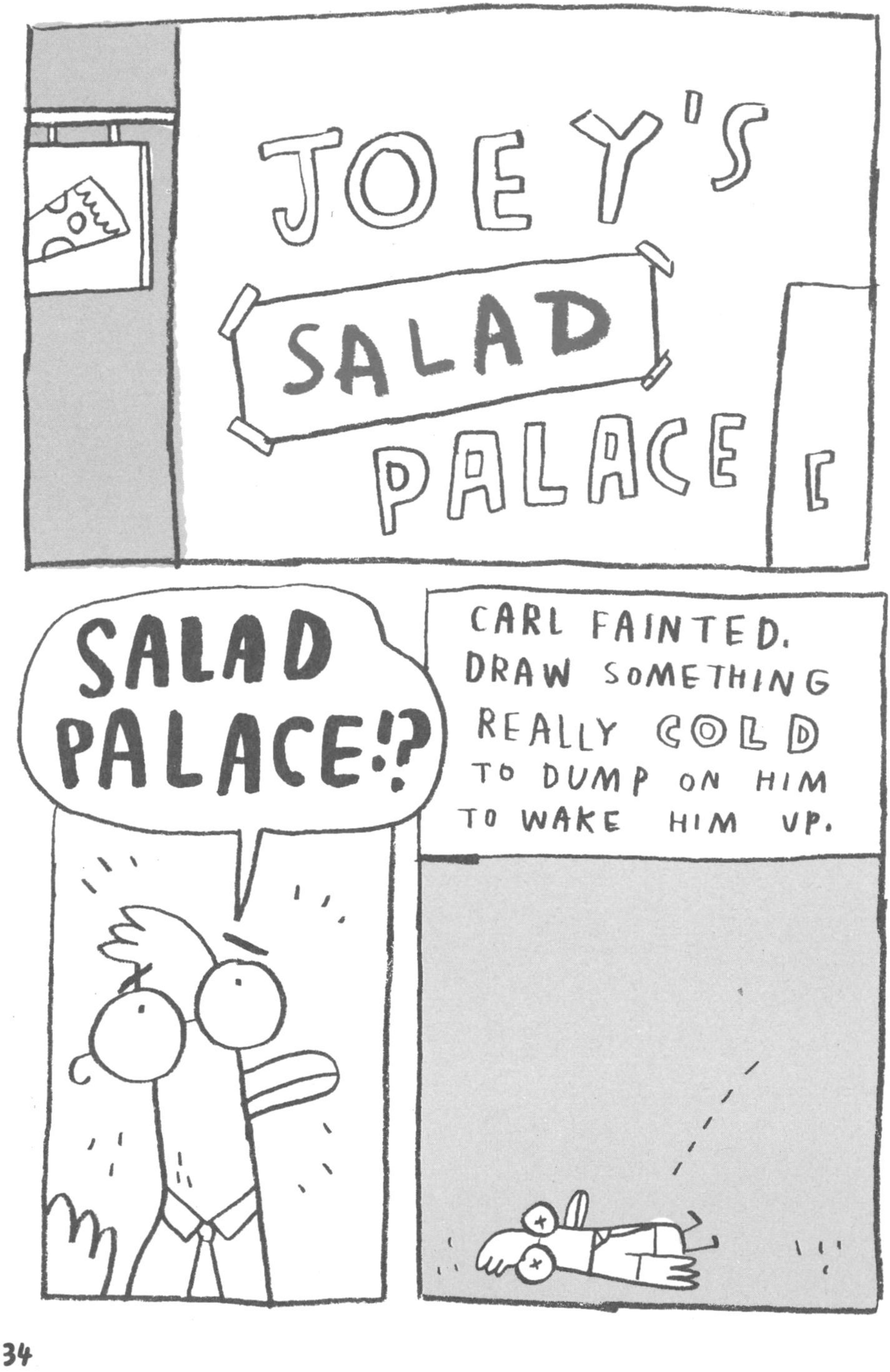
JOEY'S
SALAD
PALACE
SALAD PALACE!?
CARL FAINTED. DRAW SOMETHING REALLY COLD TO DUMP ON HIM TO WAKE HIM UP.

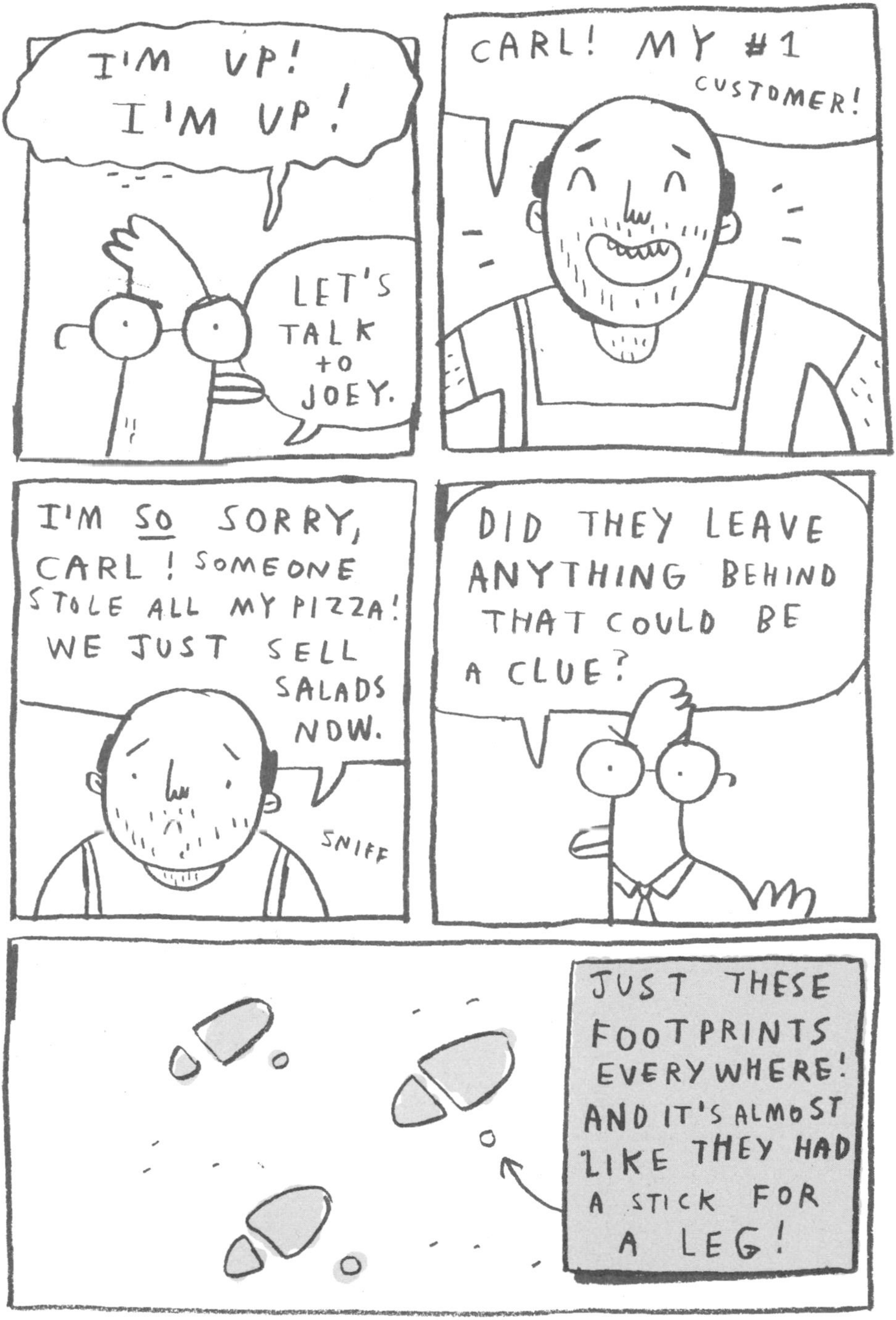
I'M UP! I'M UP!
LET'S TALK to JOEY.
CARL! MY #1 CUSTOMER!
I'M SO SORRY, CARL! SOMEONE STOLE ALL MY PIZZA! WE JUST SELL SALADS NOW.
SNIFF
DID THEY LEAVE ANYTHING BEHIND THAT COULD BE A CLUE?
JUST THESE FOOTPRINTS EVERYWHERE! AND IT'S ALMOST LIKE THEY HAD A STICK FOR A LEG!

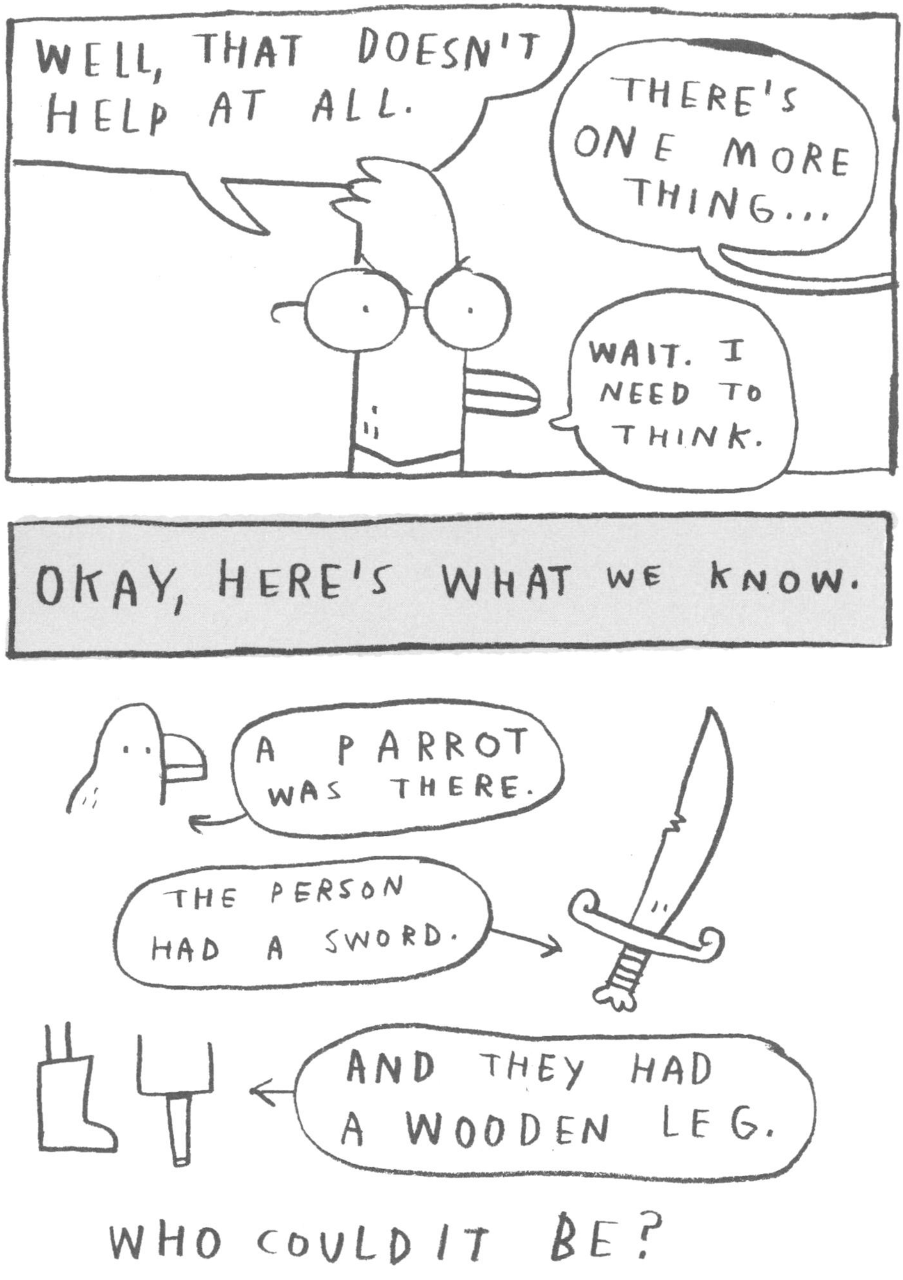
WELL, THAT DOESN'T HELP AT ALL.
THERE'S ONE MORE THING...
WAIT. I NEED TO THINK.
OKAY, HERE'S WHAT WE KNOW.
A PARROT WAS THERE.
THE PERSON HAD A SWORD.
AND THEY HAD A WOODEN LEG.
WHO COULD IT BE?

IT'S PROBABLY NOT:

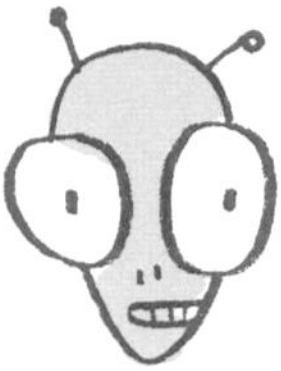

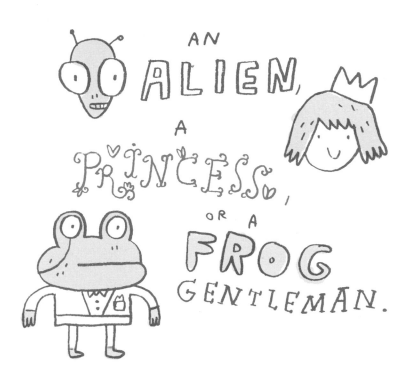

AN ALIEN,

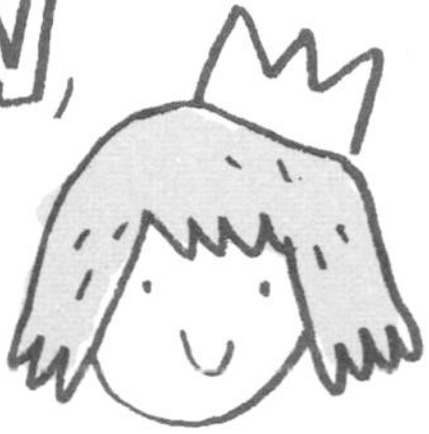

A PRINCESS,

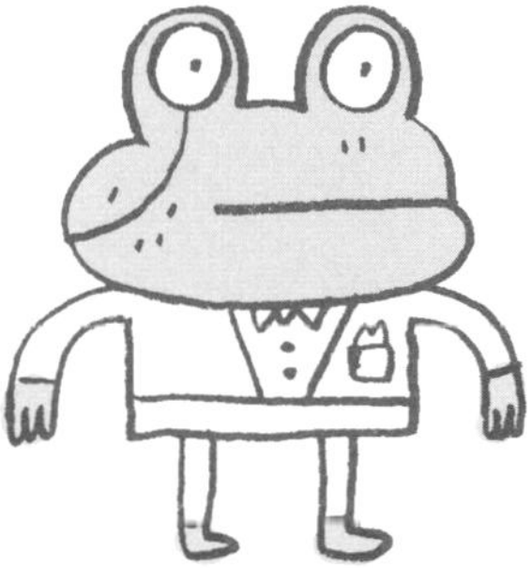

OR A FROG GENTLEMAN.

HMMMMM.

ANY IDEAS?

WRITE YOUR IDEA HERE

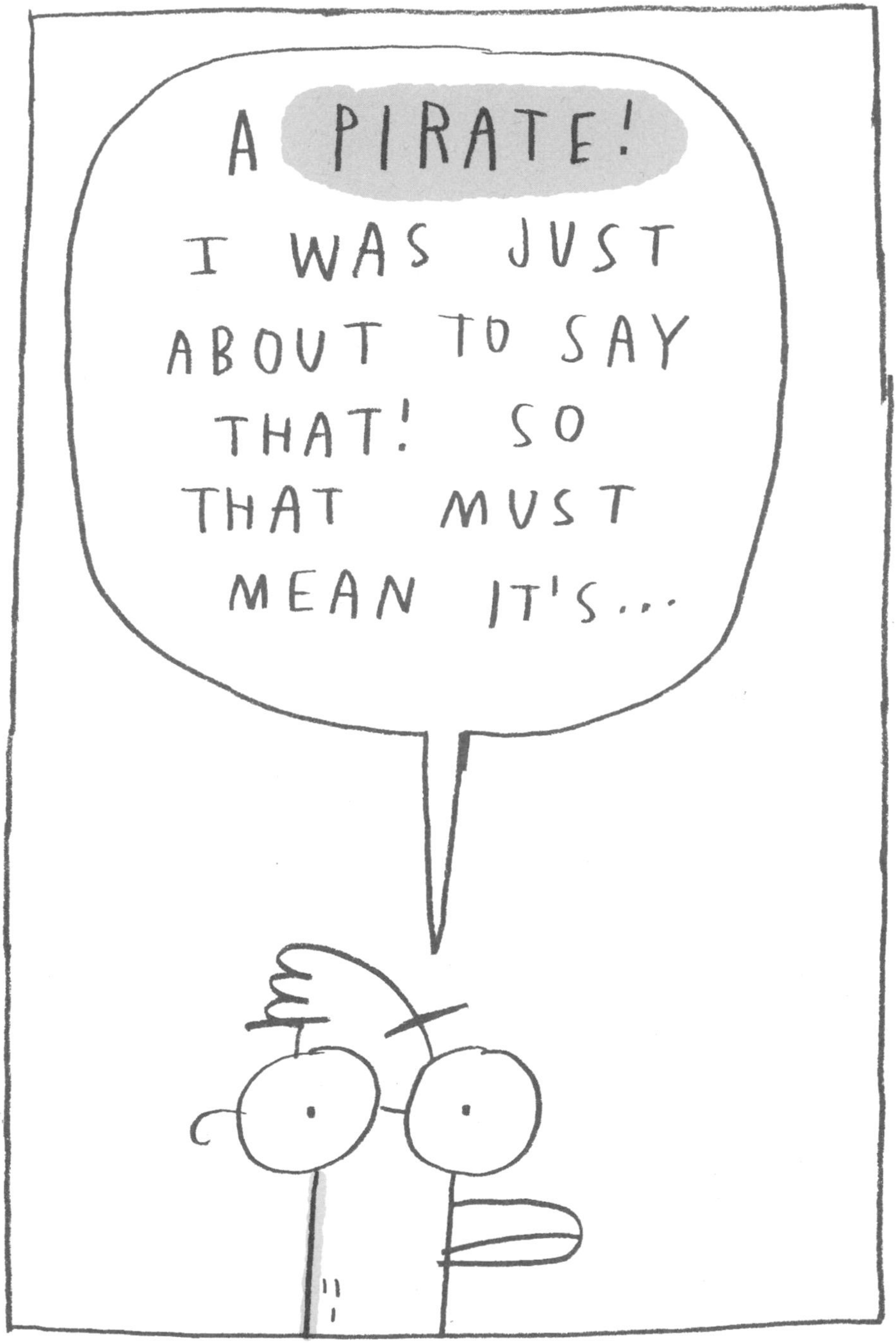
A PIRATE! I WAS JUST ABOUT TO SAY THAT! SO THAT MUST MEAN IT'S...

THE DREAD PIRATE SLOBBERTS

(THE MEANEST, NASTIEST PIRATE EVER TO SAIL THE SEVEN SEAS).

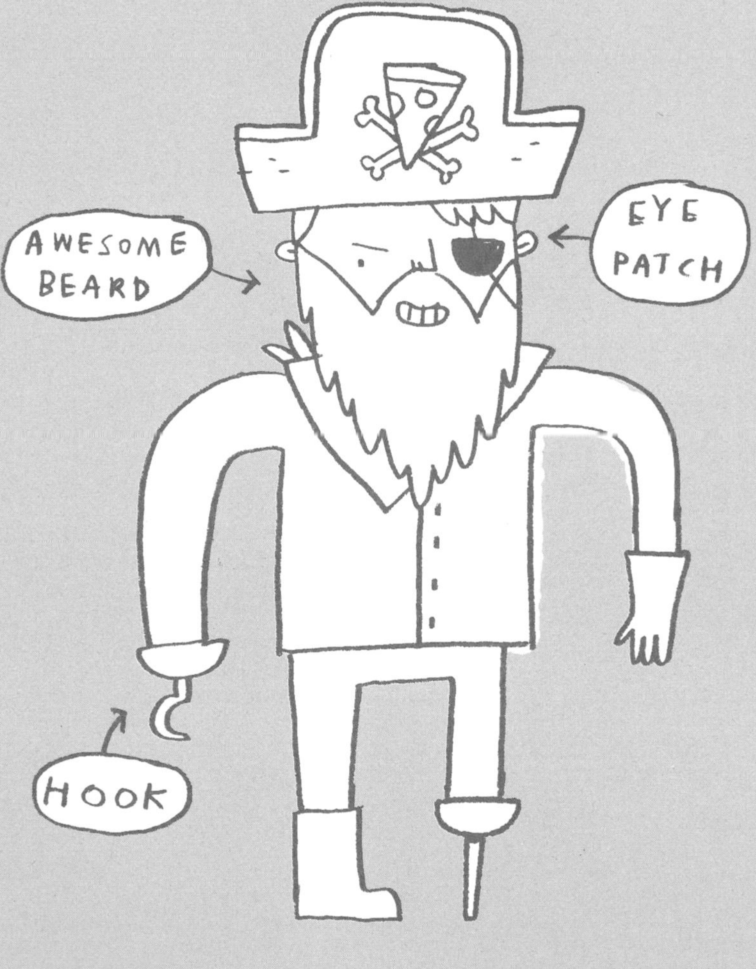
AWESOME BEARD
EYE PATCH
HOOK

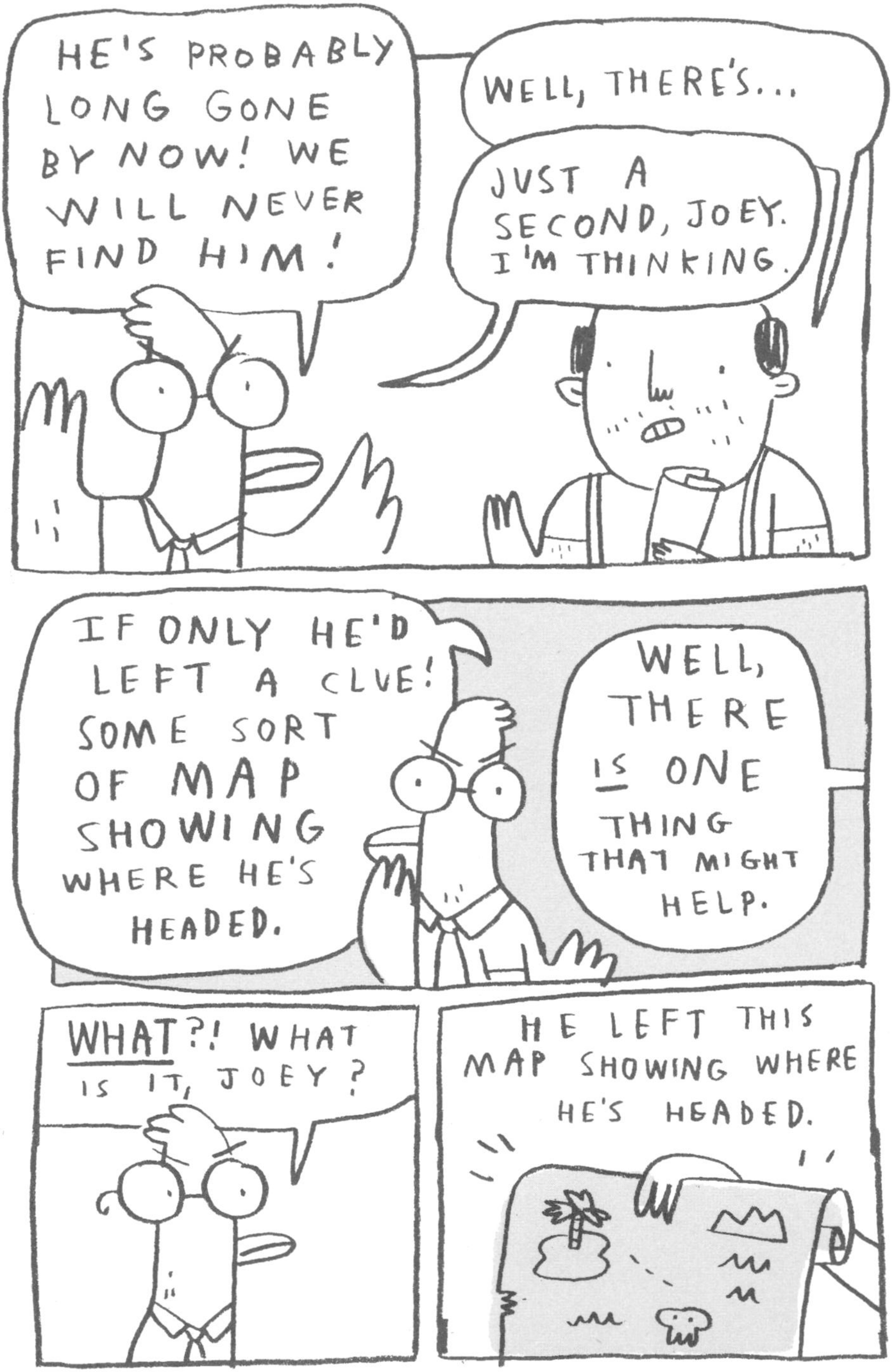
HE'S PROBABLY LONG GONE BY NOW! WE WILL NEVER FIND HIM!
WELL, THERE'S...
JUST A SECOND, JOEY. I'M THINKING.
IF ONLY HE'D LEFT A CLUE! SOME SORT OF MAP SHOWING WHERE HE'S HEADED.
WELL, THERE IS ONE THING THAT MIGHT HELP.
WHAT?! WHAT IS IT, JOEY?
HE LEFT THIS MAP SHOWING WHERE HE'S HEADED.

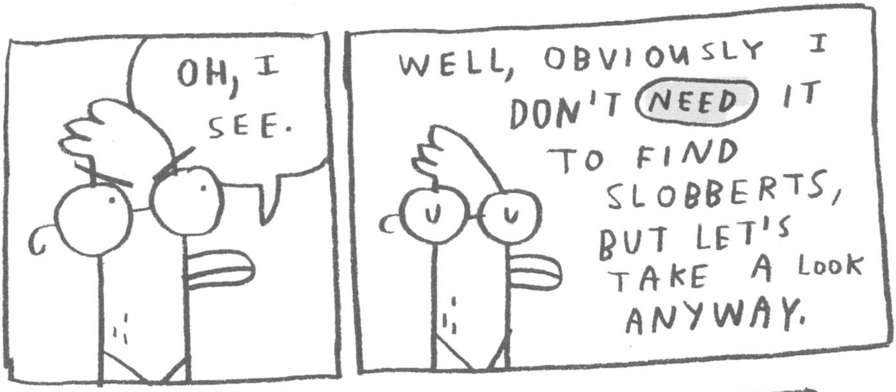
OH, I SEE.
WELL, OBVIOUSLY I DON'T NEED IT TO FIND SLOBBERTS, BUT LET'S TAKE A LOOK ANYWAY.

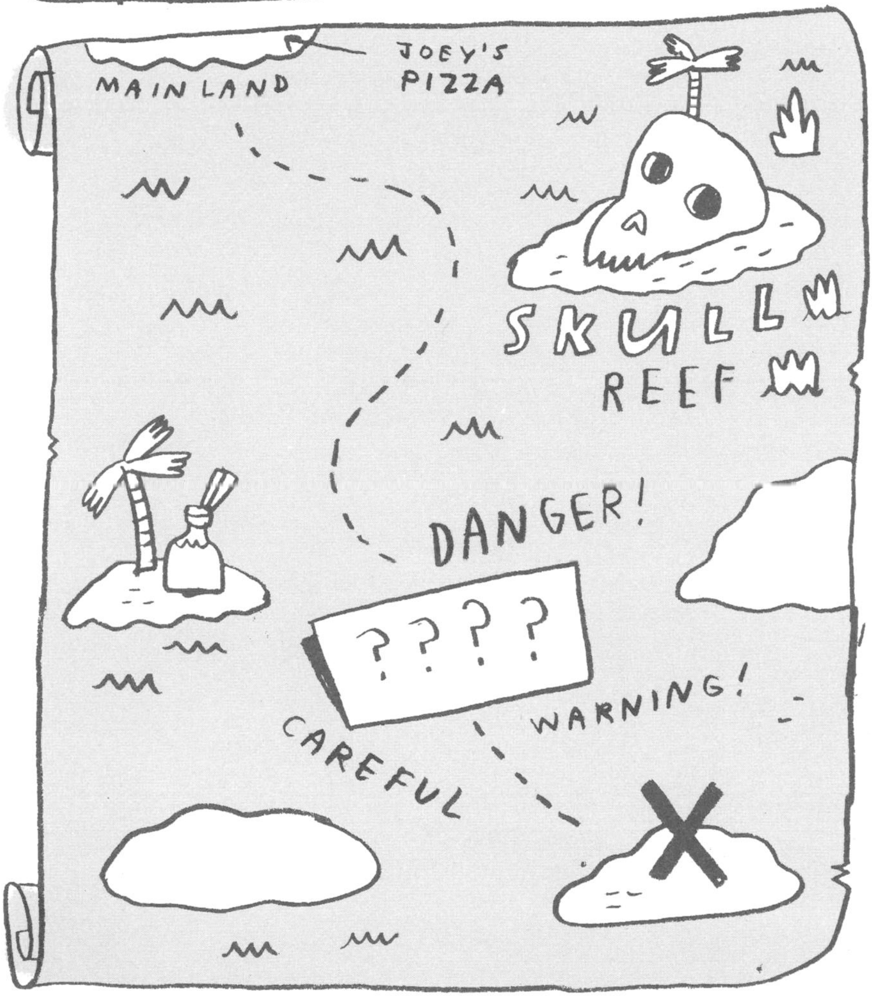
JOEY'S PIZZA
MAINLAND
SKULL REEF
DANGER!
????
WARNING!
CAREFUL

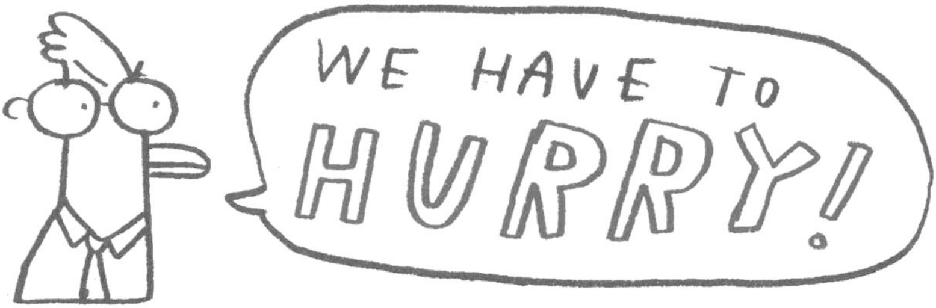
WE HAVE TO HURRY!

LET'S PACK A FEW THINGS FOR THE MISSION:

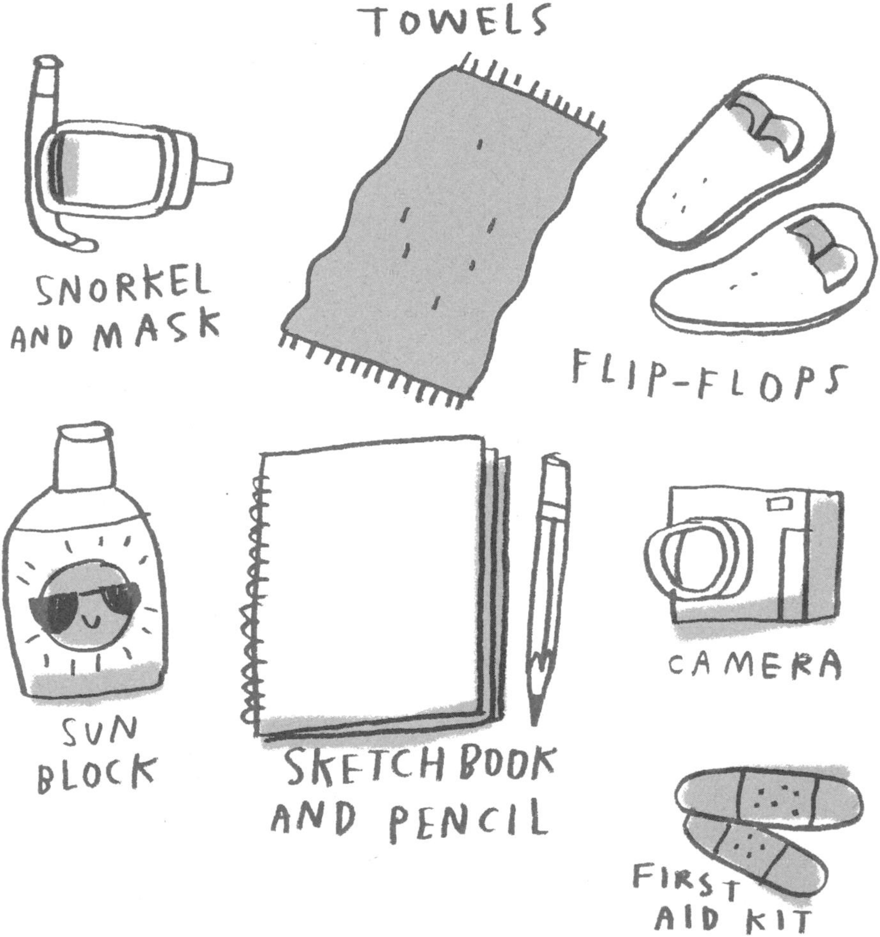
TOWELS
SNORKEL AND MASK
FLIP-FLOPS
SUN BLOCK
SKETCHBOOK AND PENCIL
CAMERA
FIRST AID KIT

WHAT ELSE SHOULD WE BRING?

AND DON'T FORGET THE SPY GEAR.

SUPERSONIC LISTENING DEVICE!

HIGH JUMPER SHOES!

SWISS ARMY BRIEFCASE!

ROCKET-POWERED SKATEBOARD!

WALKIE-TALKIES!

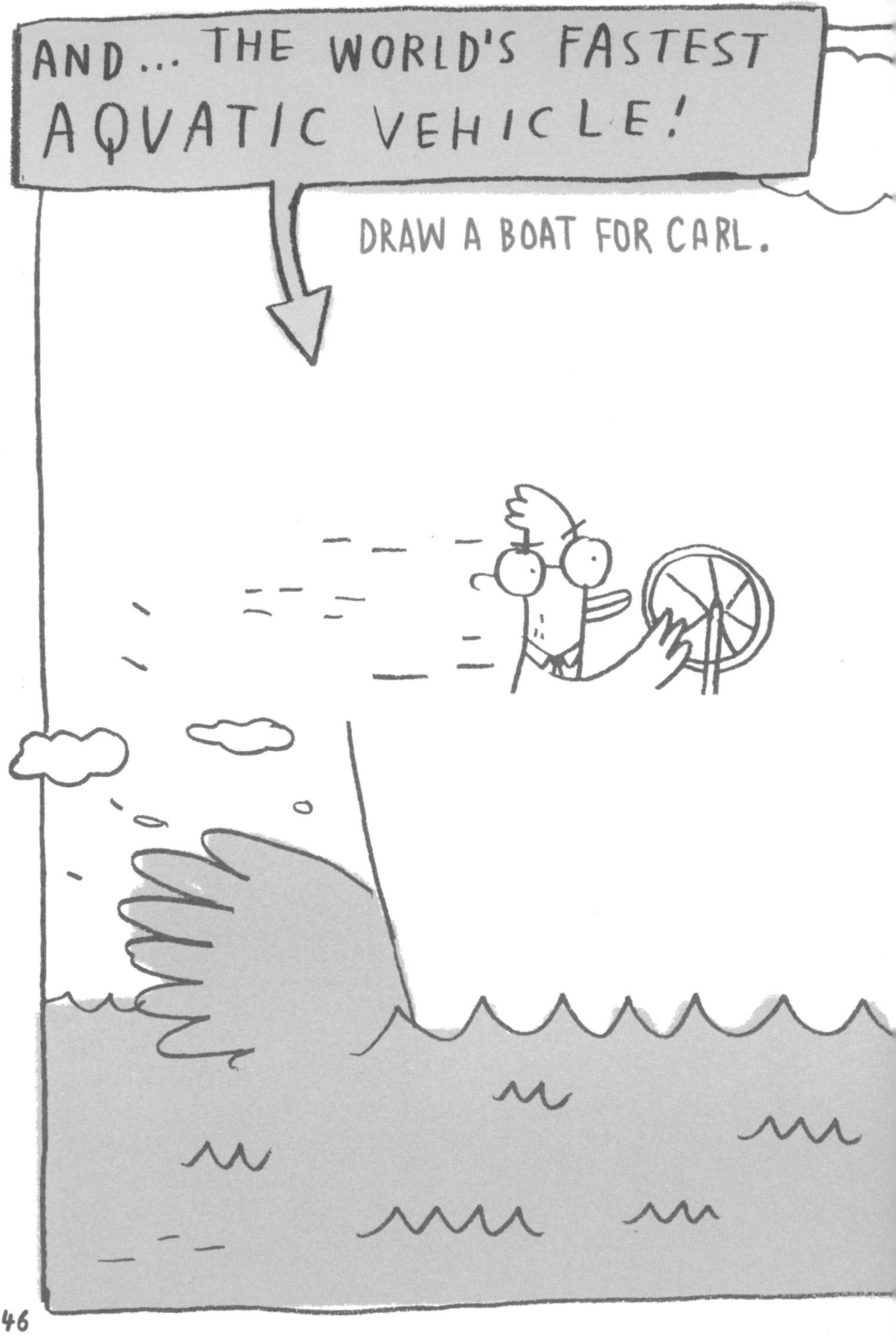
AND... THE WORLD'S FASTEST AQUATIC VEHICLE!
DRAW A BOAT FOR CARL.

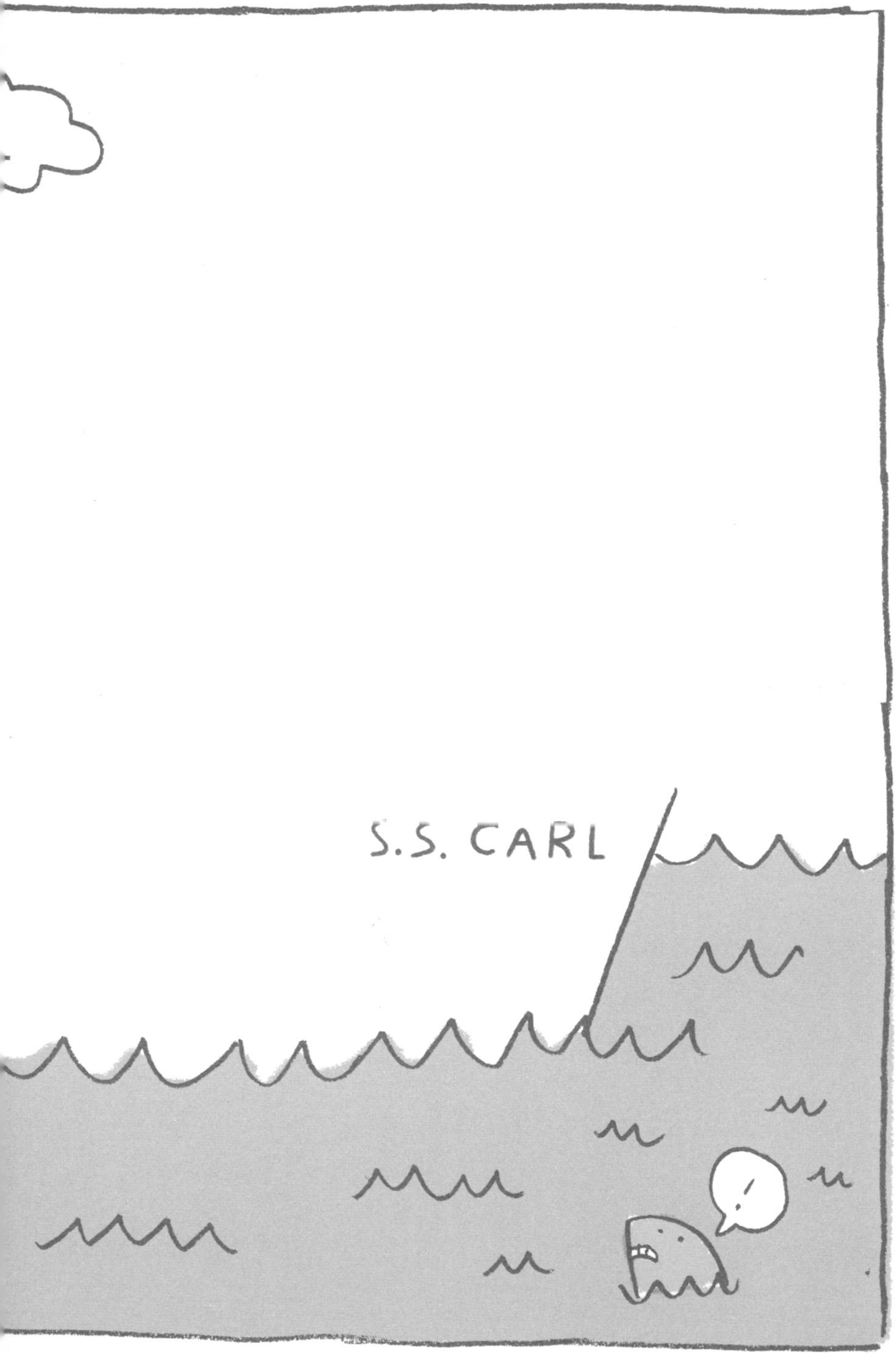
S.S. CARL
!

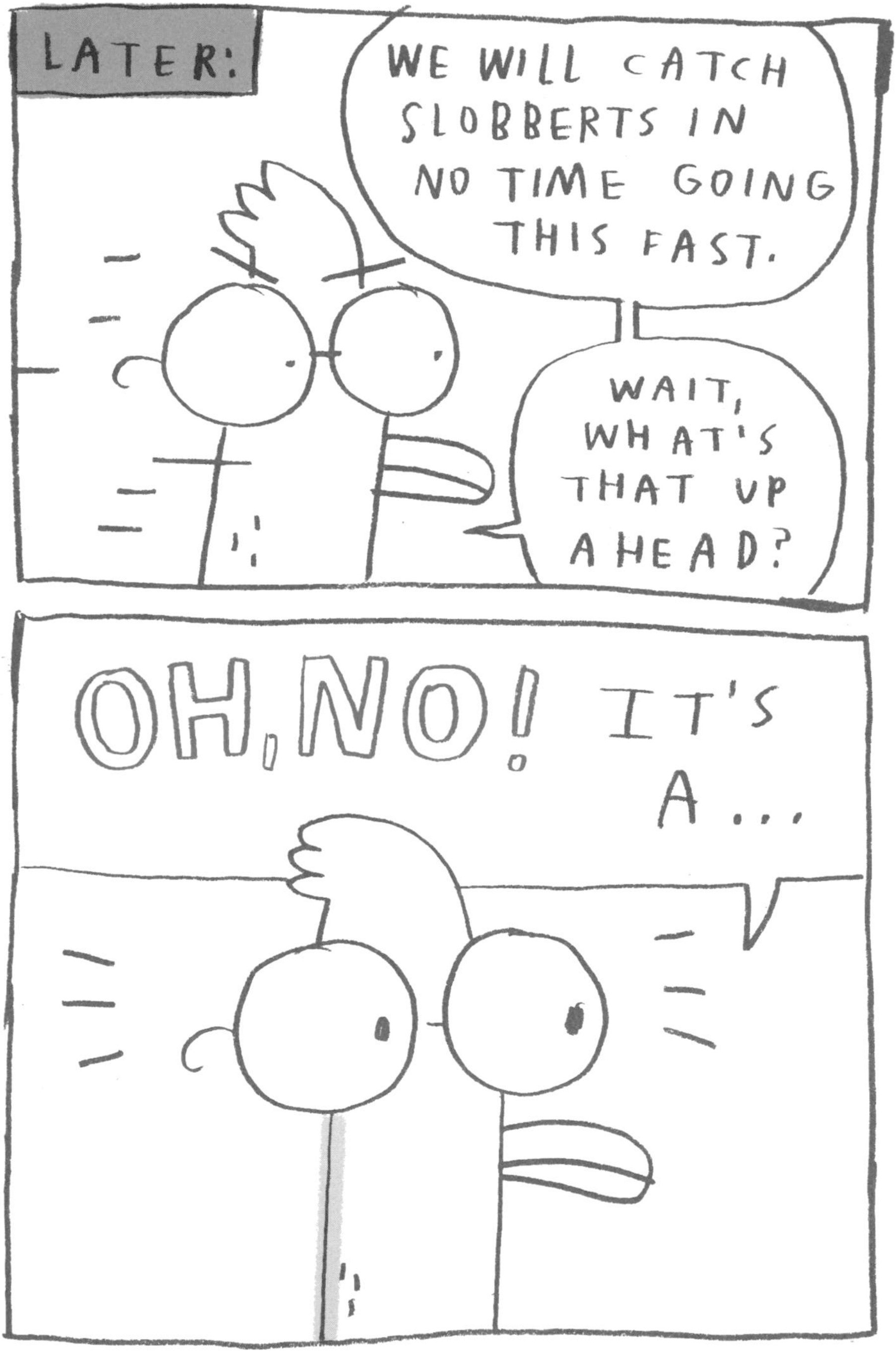
LATER:
WE WILL CATCH SLOBBERTS IN NO TIME GOING THIS FAST.
WAIT, WHAT'S THAT UP AHEAD?
OH, NO! IT'S A...

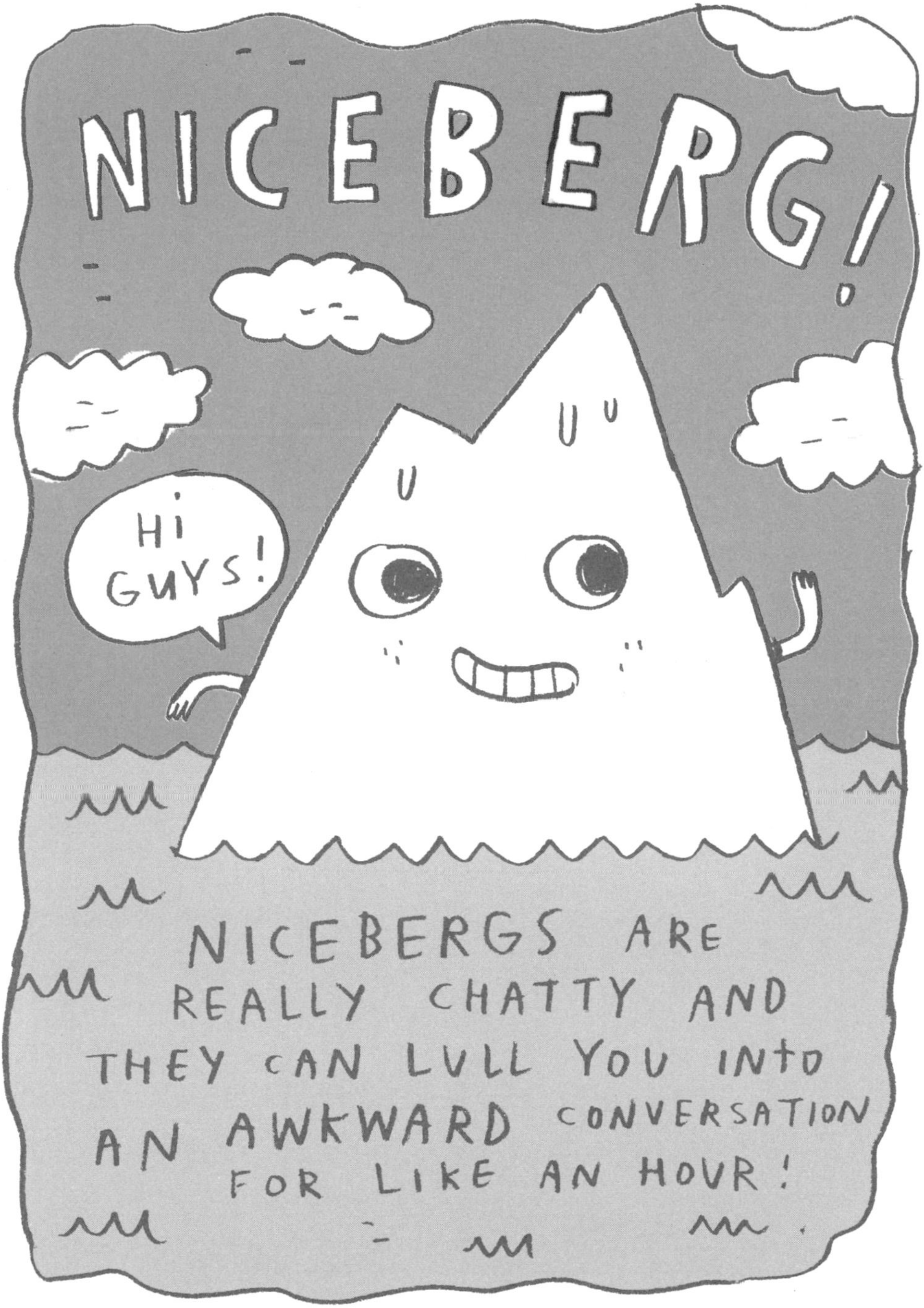
NICEBERG!
HI GUYS!
NICEBERGS ARE REALLY CHATTY AND THEY CAN LULL YOU INTO AN AWKWARD CONVERSATION FOR LIKE AN HOUR!

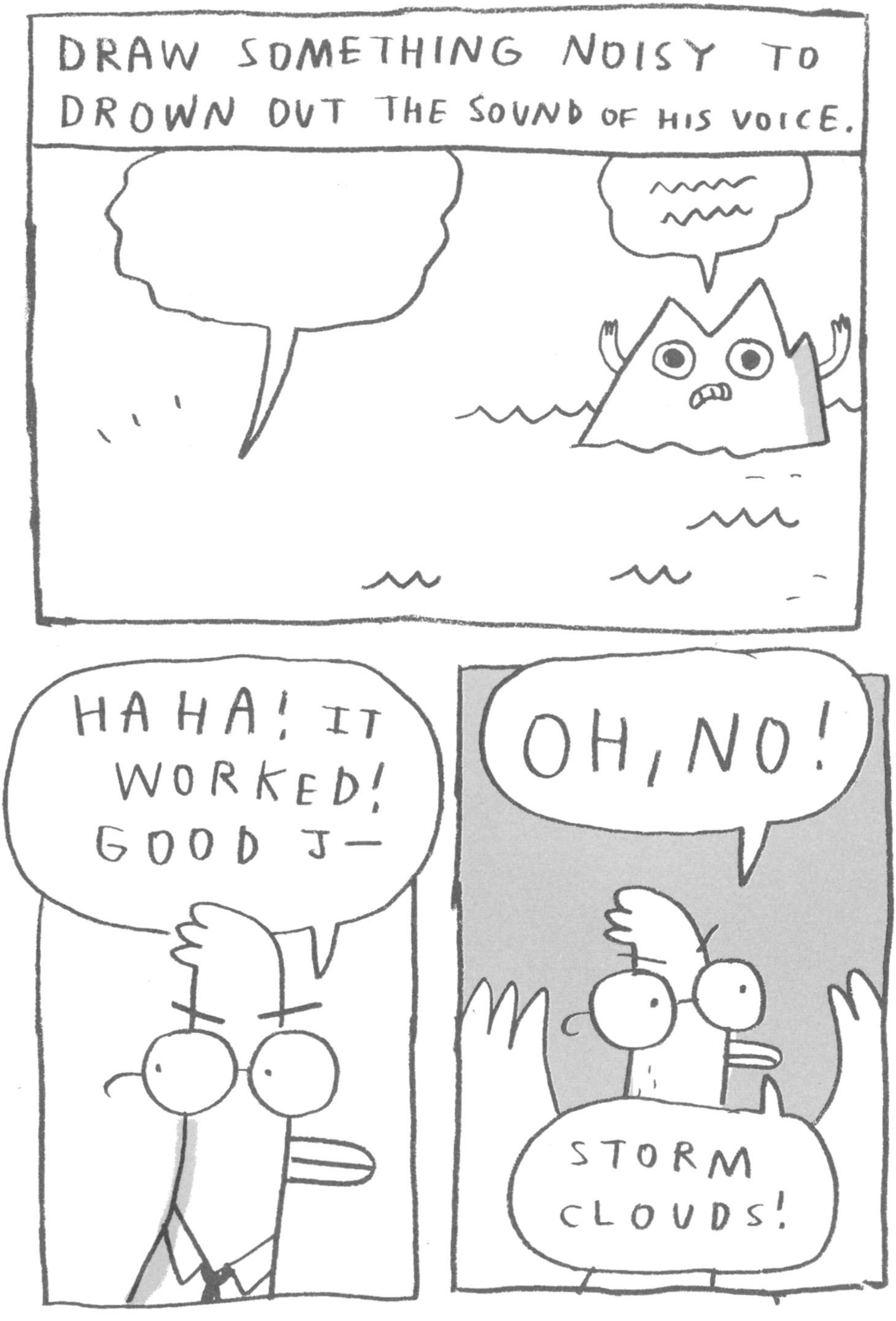
DRAW SOMETHING NOISY TO DROWN OUT THE SOUND OF HIS VOICE.
HAHA! IT WORKED! GOOD J—
OH, NO!
STORM CLOUDS!

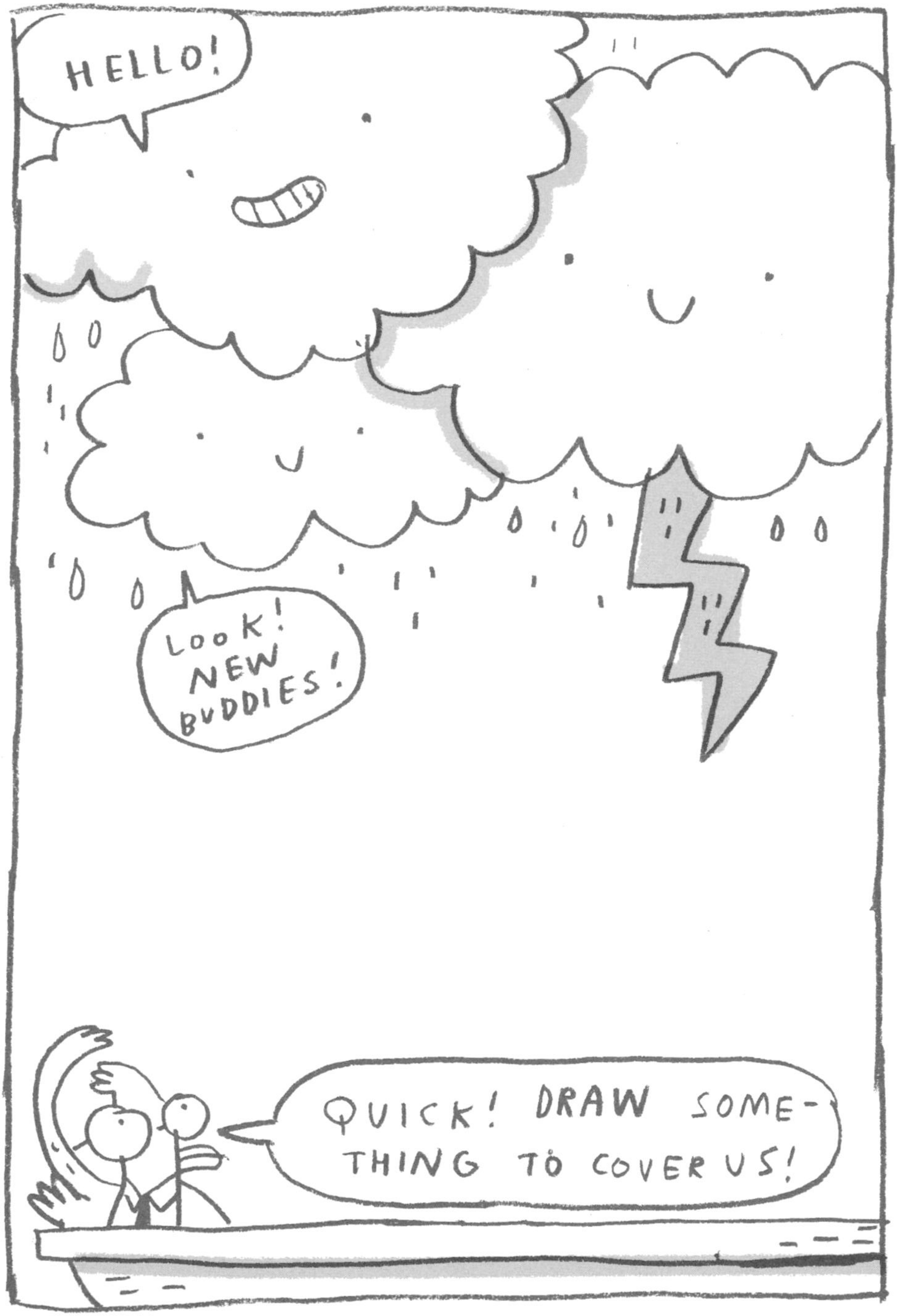
HELLO!
LOOK! NEW BUDDIES!
QUICK! DRAW SOME-THING TO COVER US!

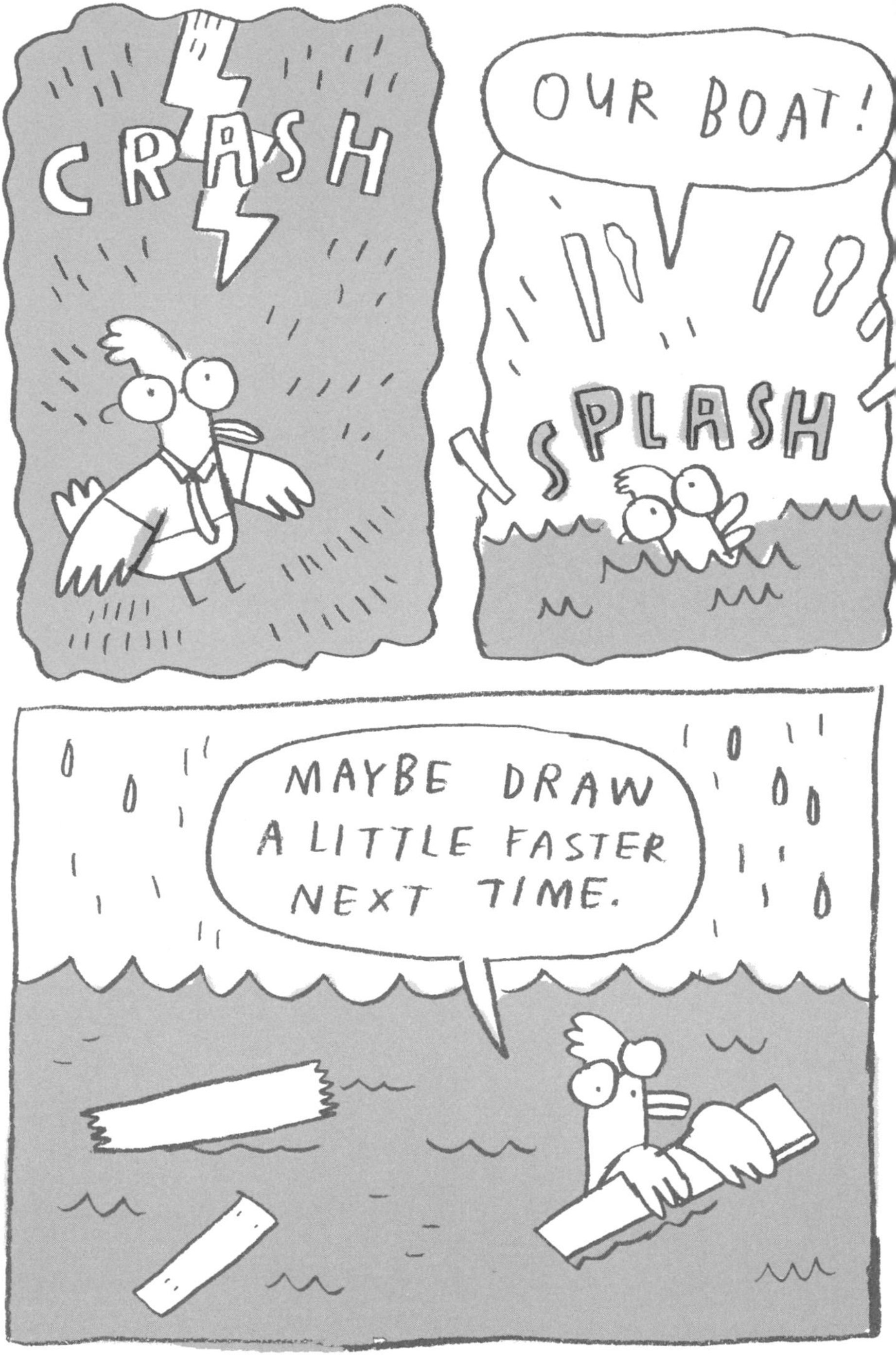
CRASH
OUR BOAT!
SPLASH
MAYBE DRAW A LITTLE FASTER NEXT TIME.

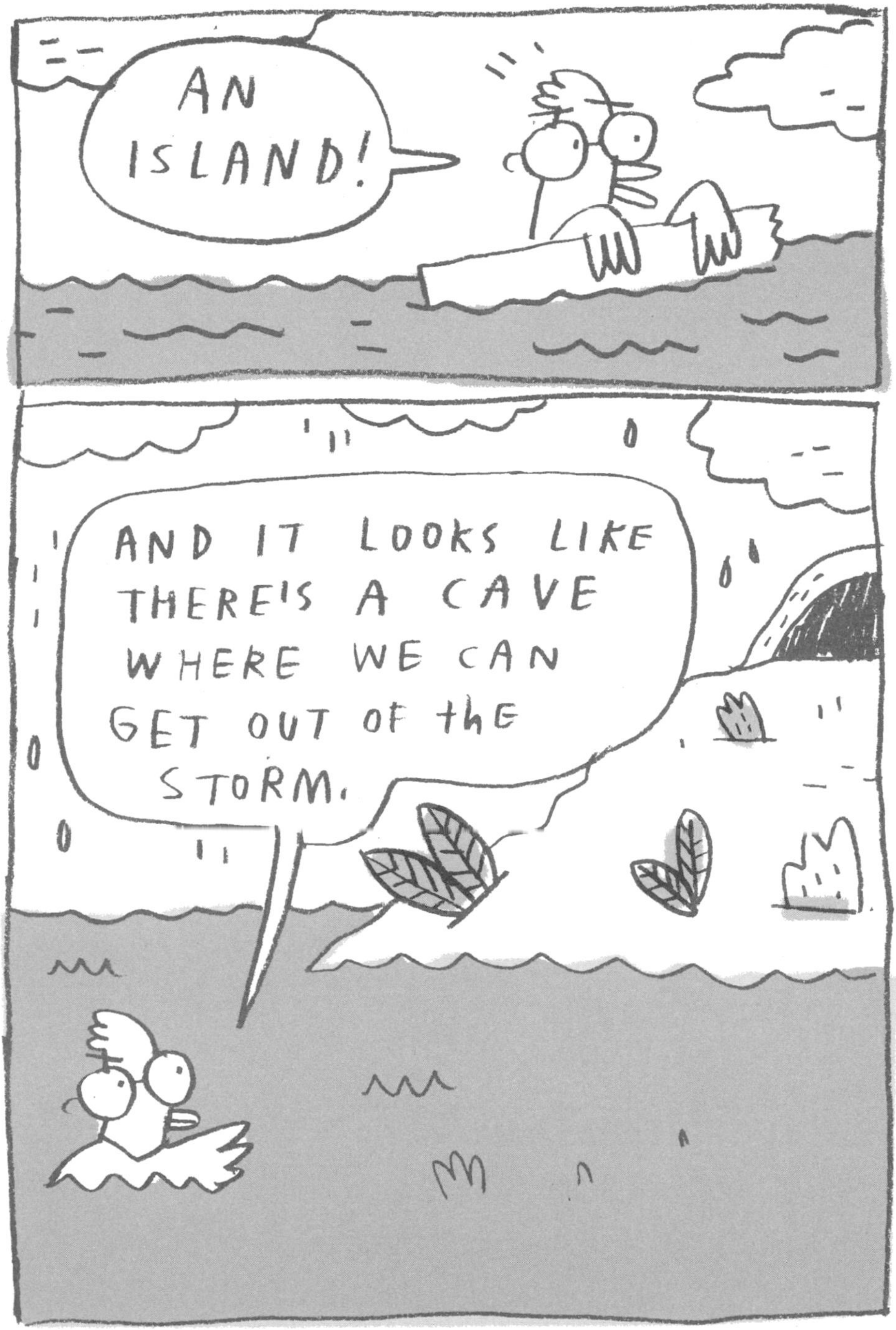
AN ISLAND!
AND IT LOOKS LIKE THERE'S A CAVE WHERE WE CAN GET OUT OF THE STORM.

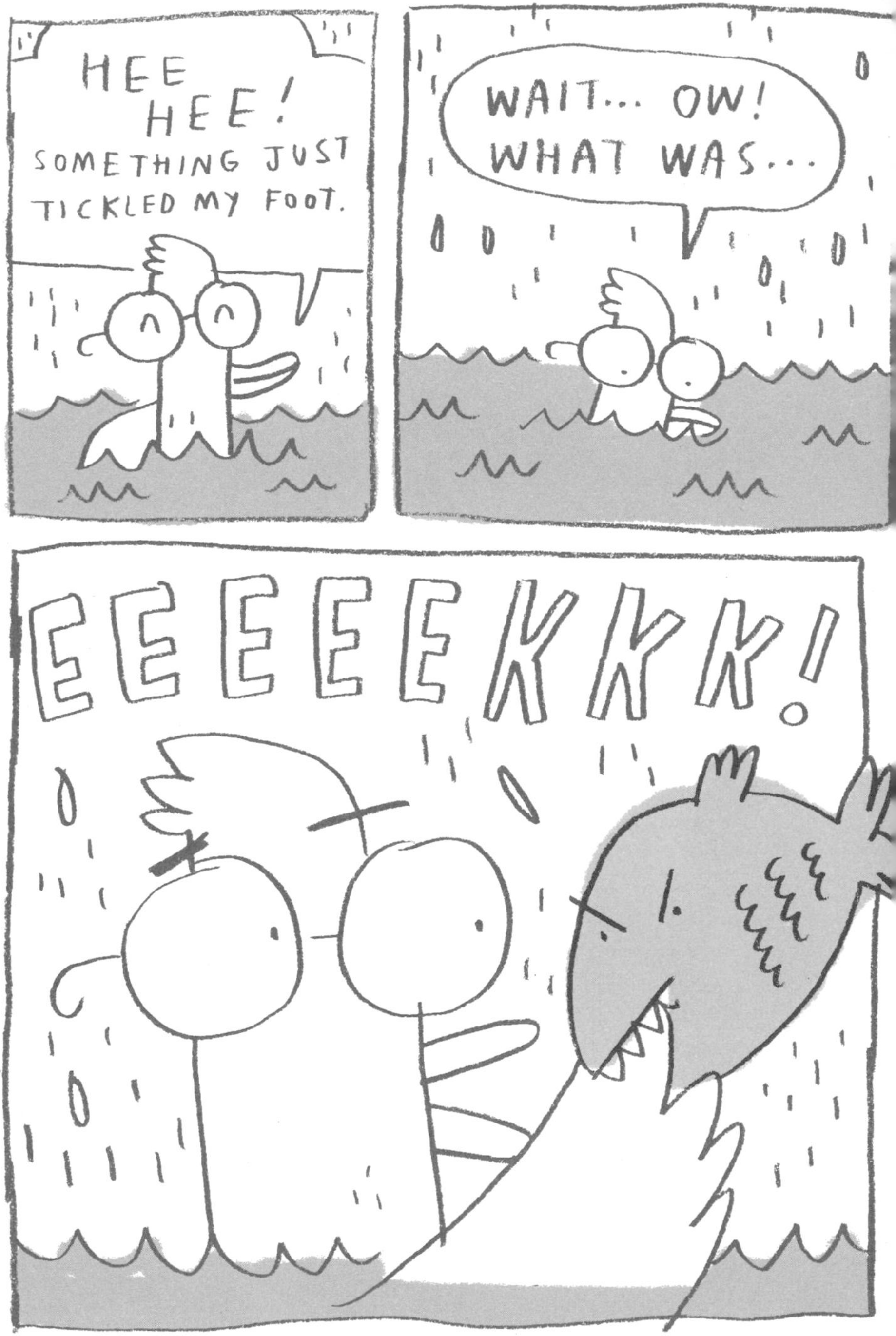
HEE HEE! SOMETHING JUST TICKLED MY FOOT.
WAIT... OW! WHAT WAS...
EEEEEKKK!

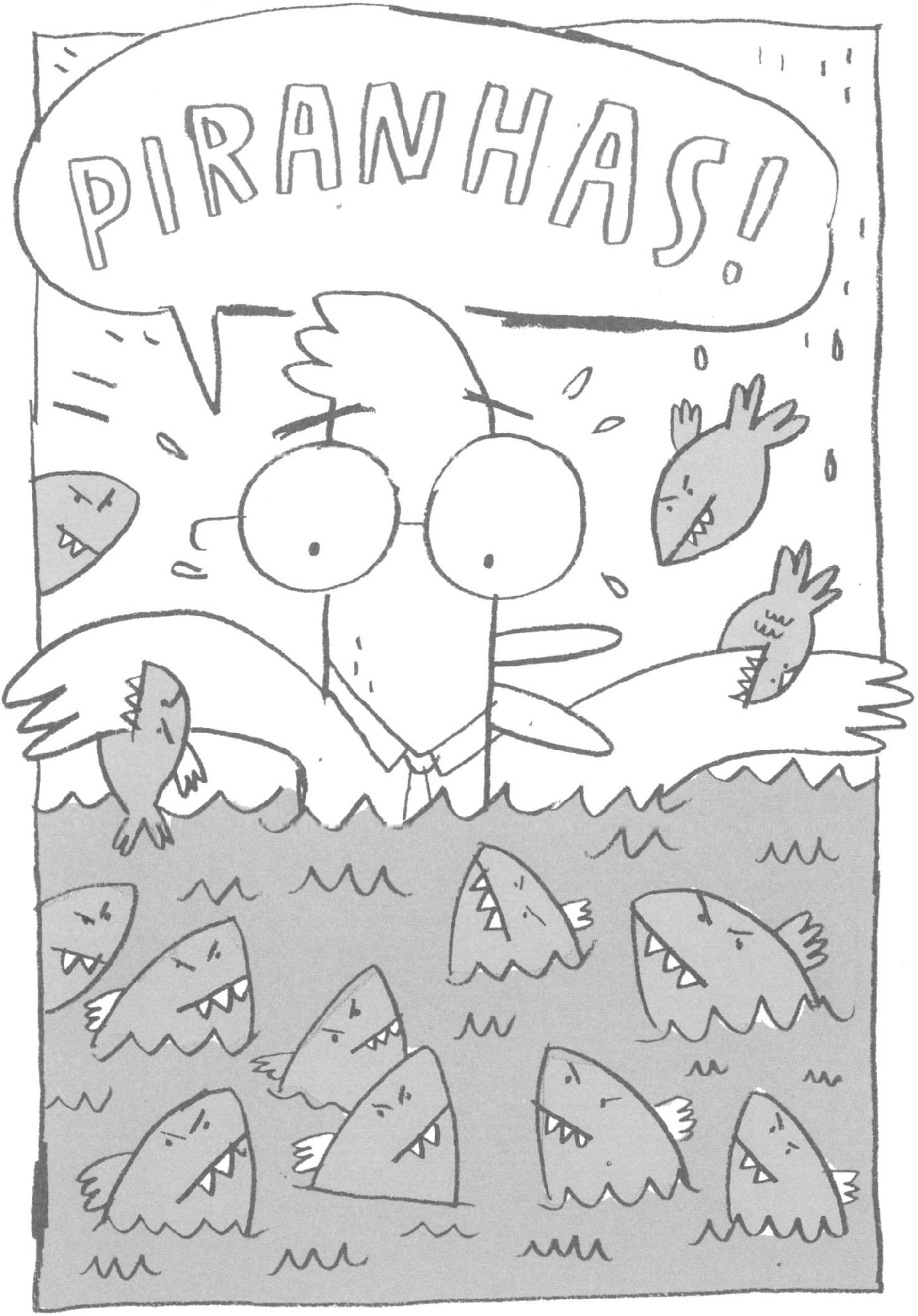
PIRANHAS!

DRAW SOMETHING REALLY **STINKY** TO MAKE THEM LEAVE!

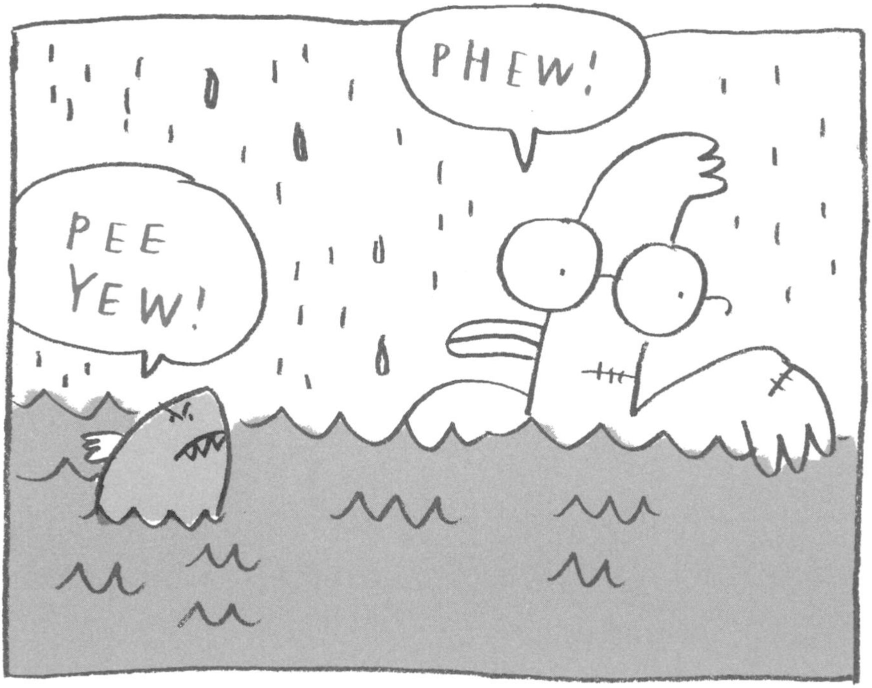
PEE YEW!
PHEW!

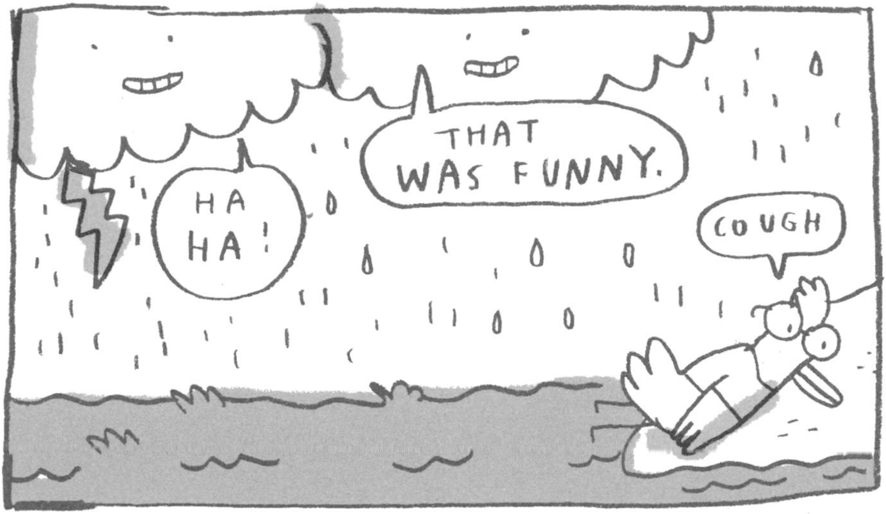
HA HA!
THAT WAS FUNNY.
COUGH

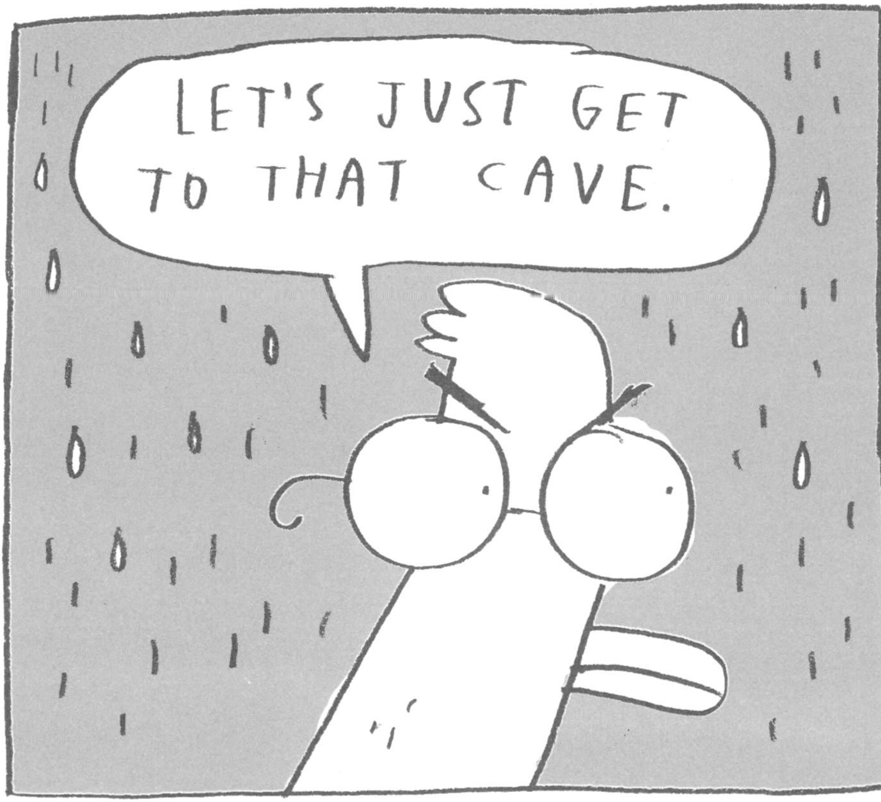
LET'S JUST GET TO THAT CAVE.

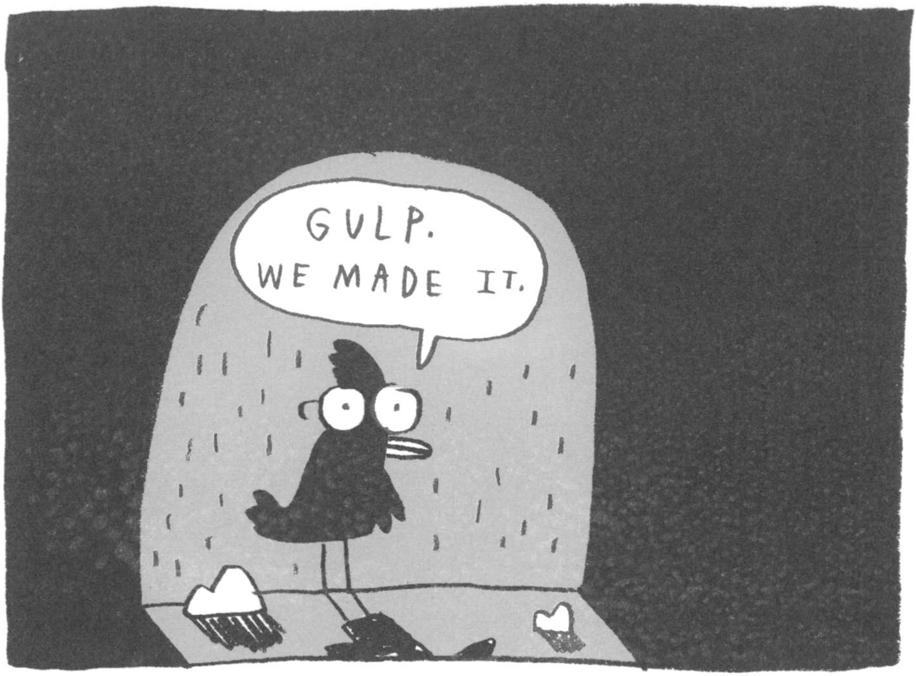
GULP.
WE MADE IT.

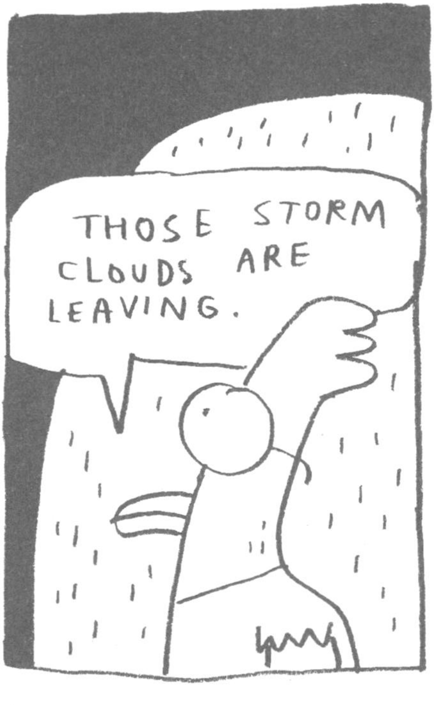
THOSE STORM CLOUDS ARE LEAVING.

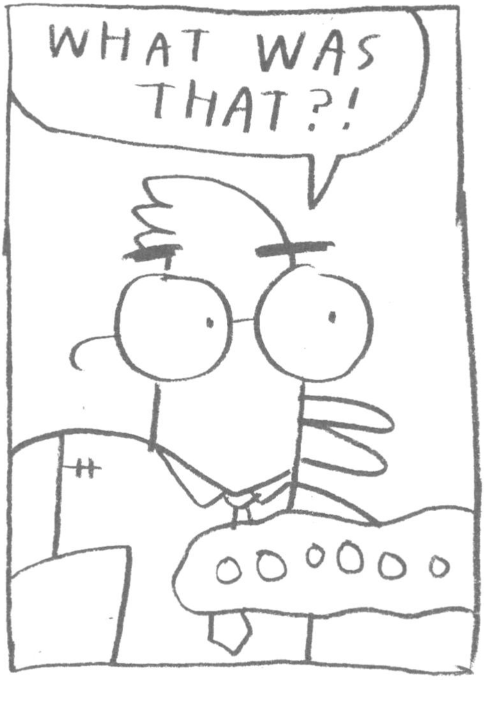
WHAT WAS THAT?!

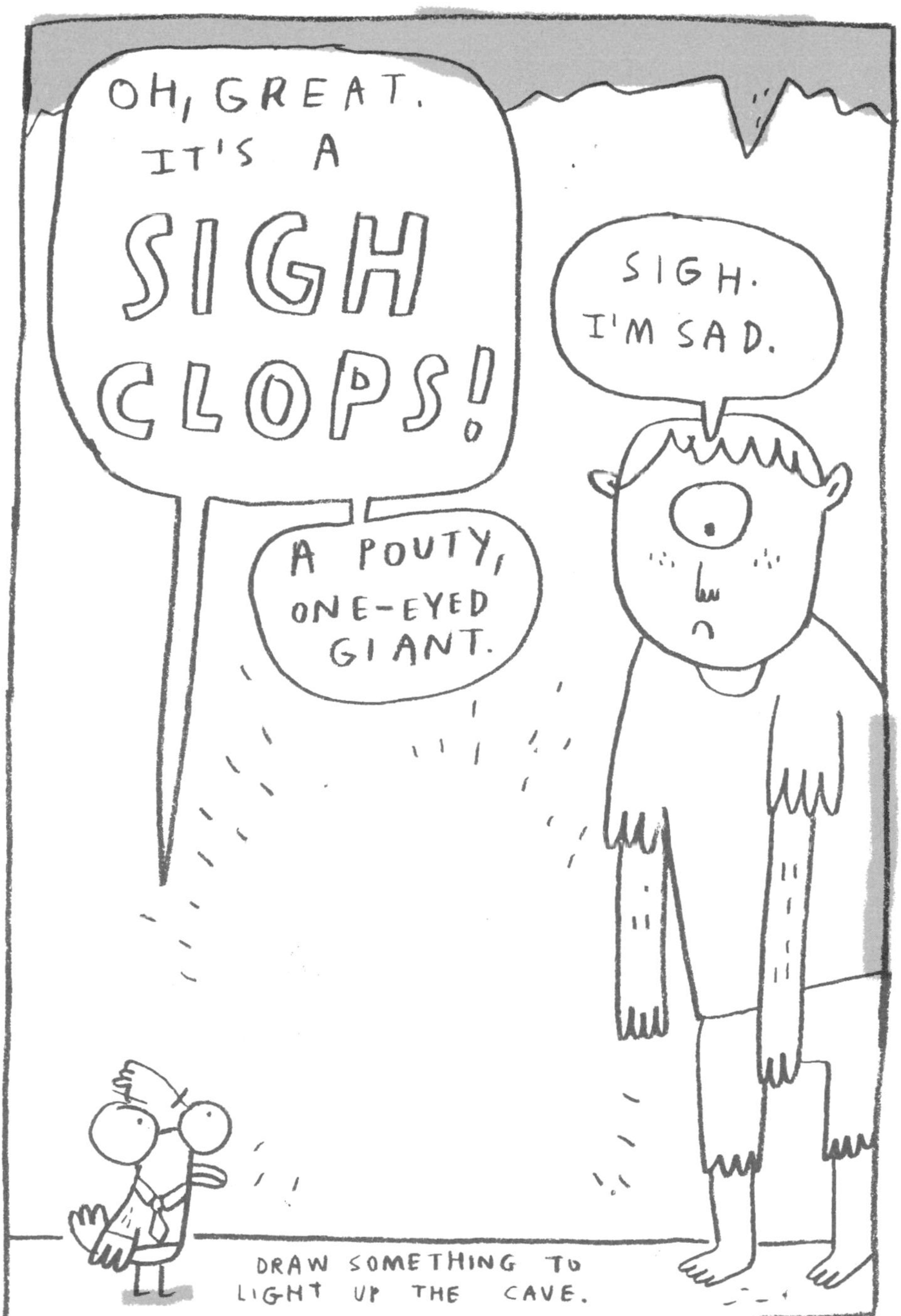
OH, GREAT. IT'S A SIGH CLOPS!
A POUTY, ONE-EYED GIANT.
SIGH. I'M SAD.
DRAW SOMETHING TO LIGHT UP THE CAVE.

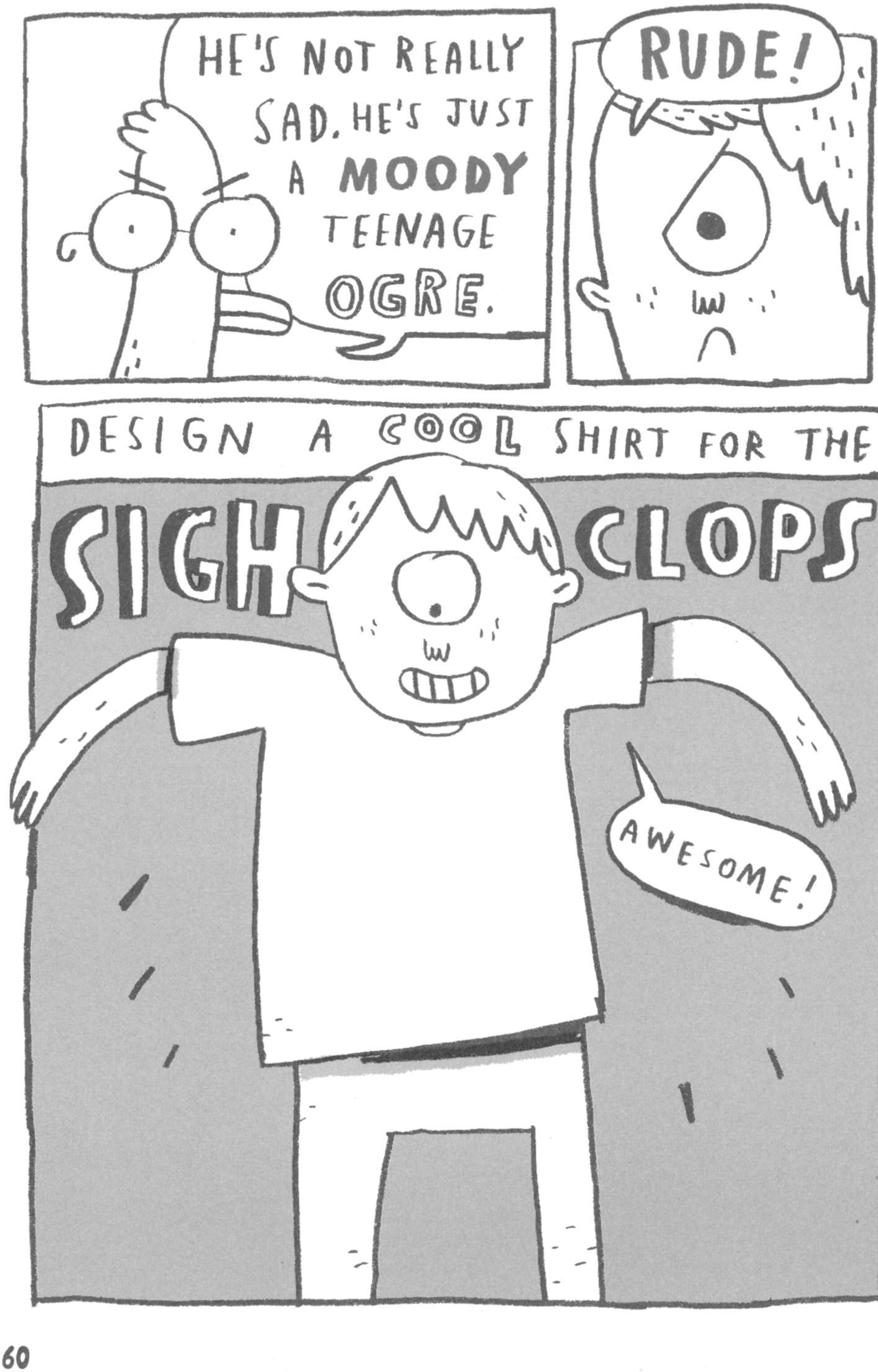
HE'S NOT REALLY SAD. HE'S JUST A **MOODY** TEENAGE OGRE.
RUDE!
DESIGN A COOL SHIRT FOR THE
SIGHCLOPS
AWESOME!

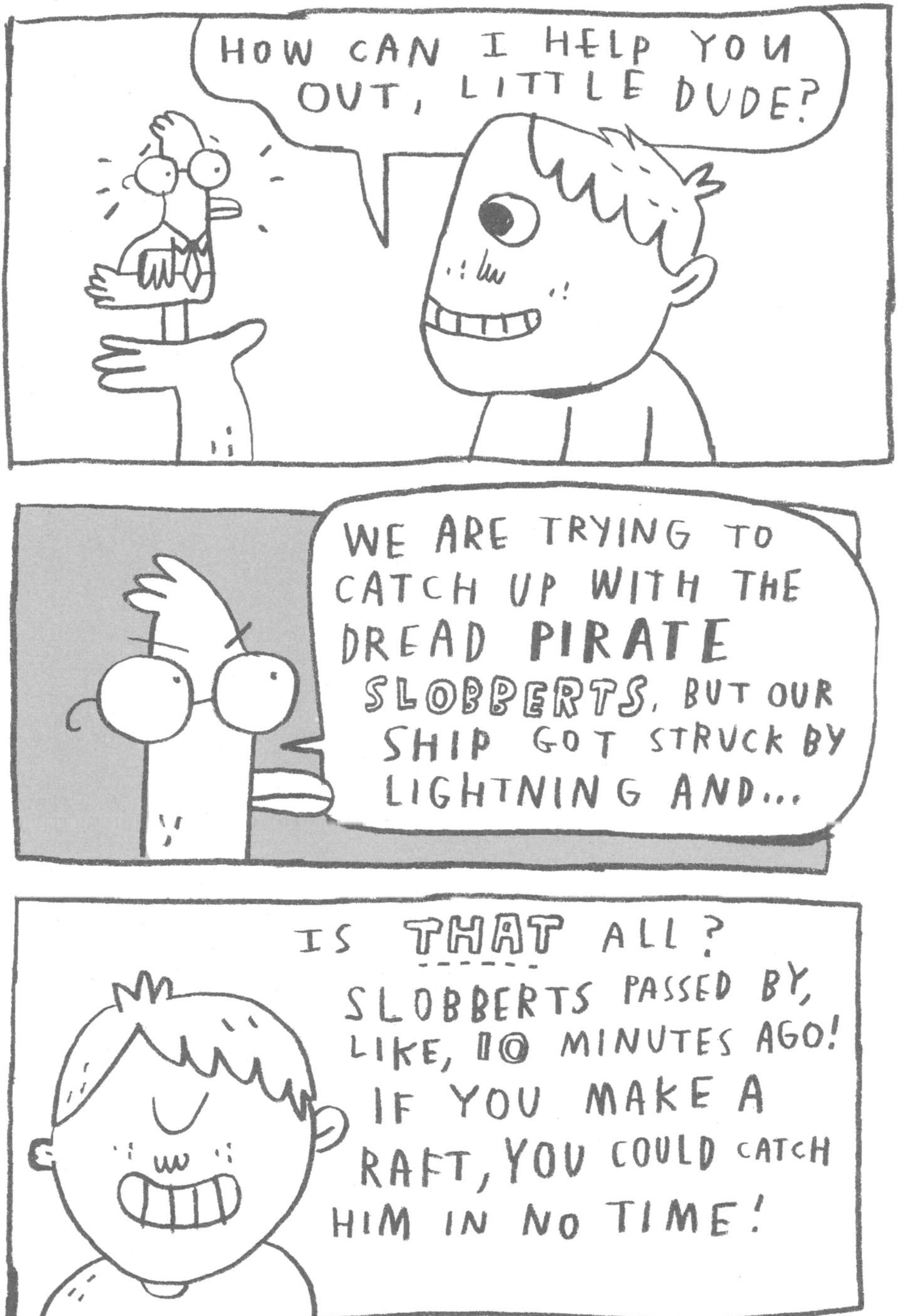
HOW CAN I HELP YOU OUT, LITTLE DUDE?
WE ARE TRYING TO CATCH UP WITH THE DREAD PIRATE SLOBBERTS, BUT OUR SHIP GOT STRUCK BY LIGHTNING AND...
IS THAT ALL? SLOBBERTS PASSED BY, LIKE, 10 MINUTES AGO! IF YOU MAKE A RAFT, YOU COULD CATCH HIM IN NO TIME!

YOU CAN USE SOME OF MY COOL STUFF TO BUILD A **RAFT**.

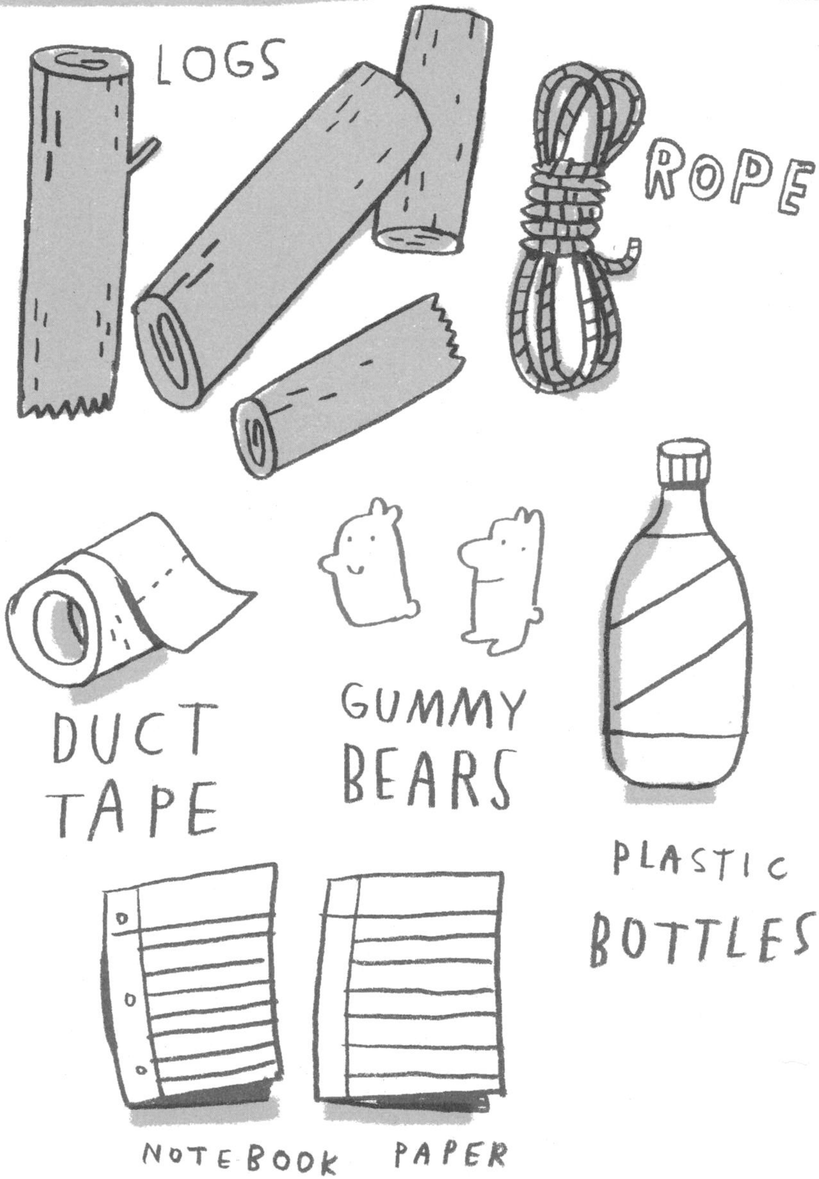
LOGS
ROPE
DUCT TAPE
GUMMY BEARS
PLASTIC BOTTLES
NOTEBOOK PAPER

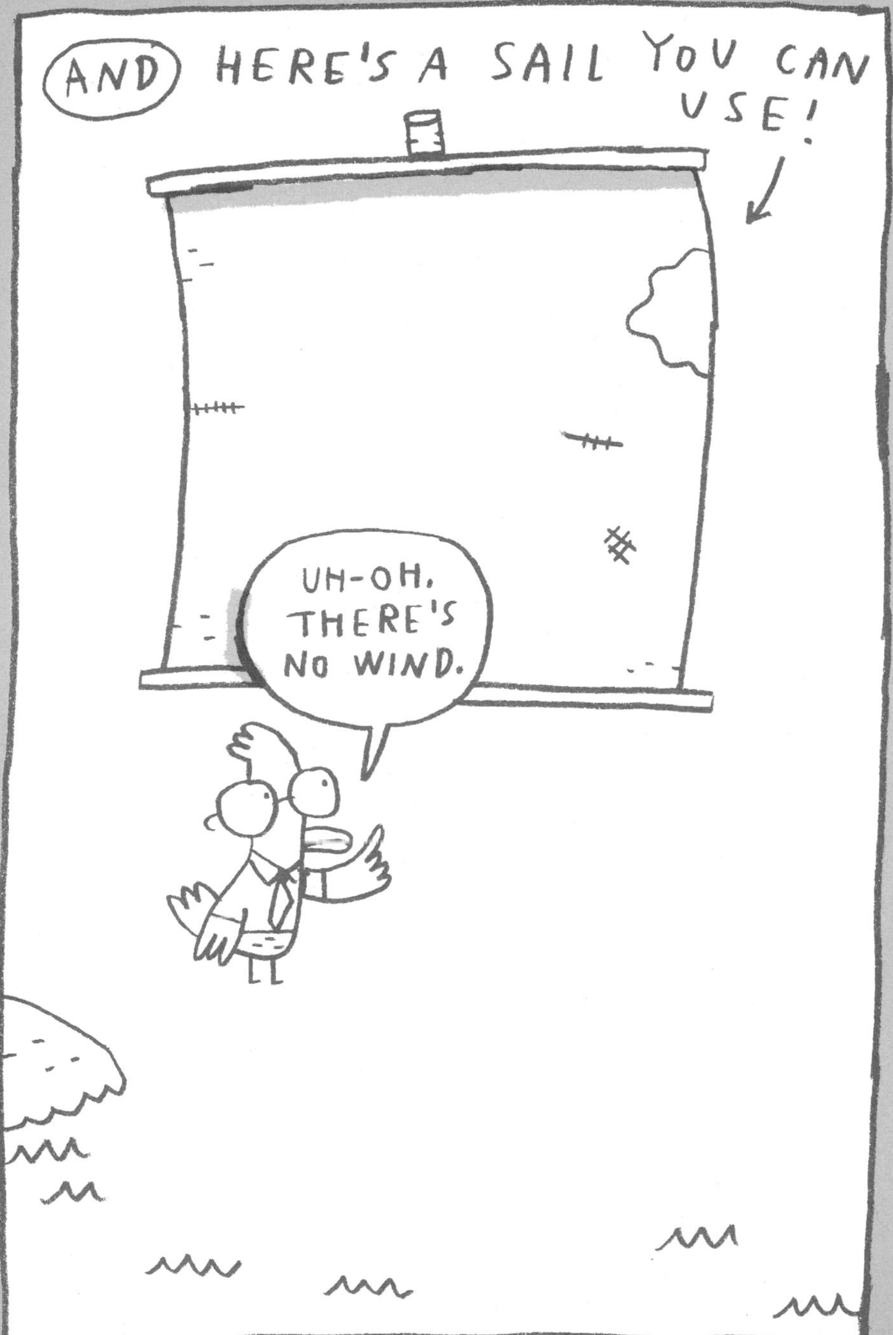
AND HERE'S A SAIL YOU CAN USE!
UH-OH. THERE'S NO WIND.

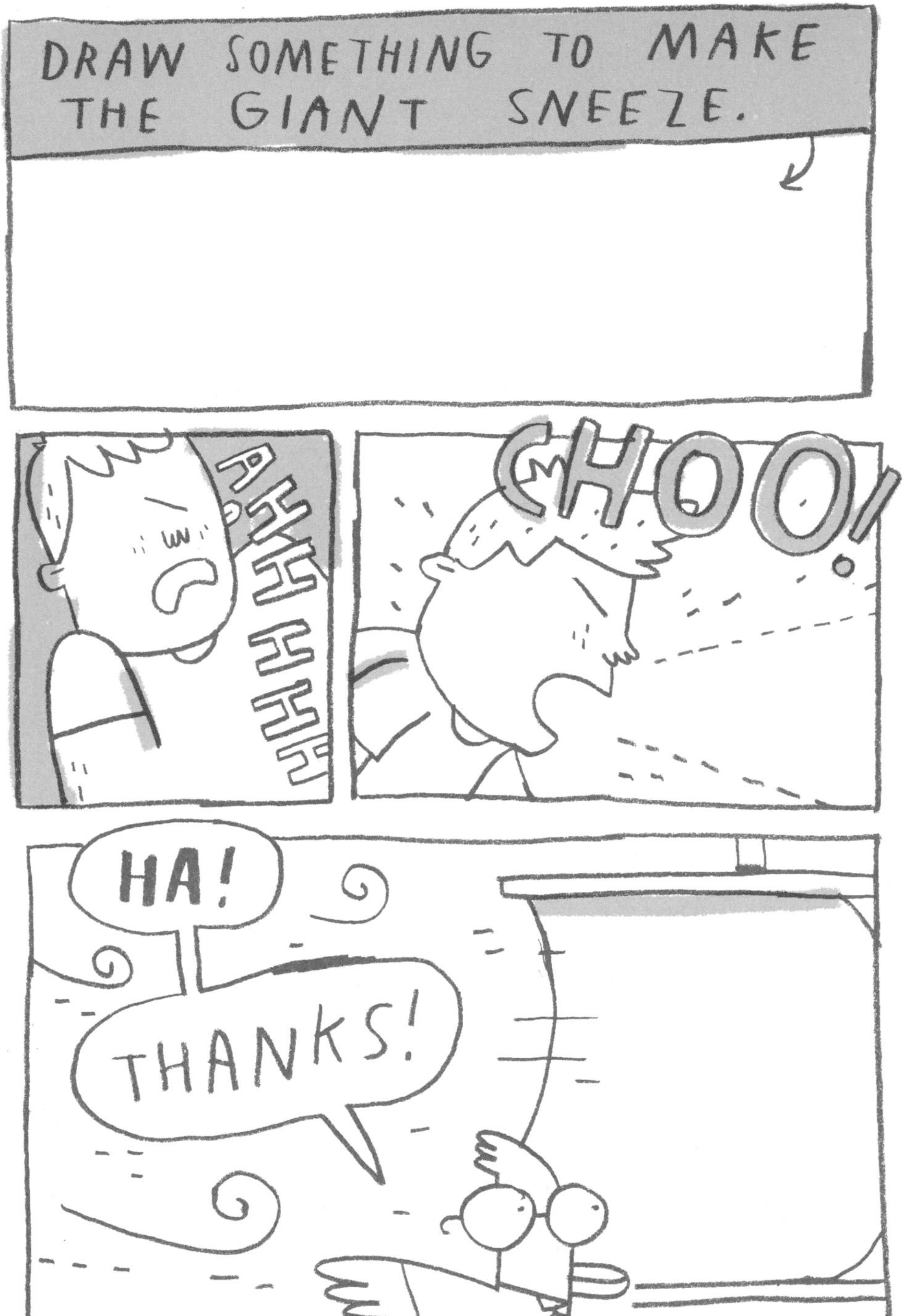
DRAW SOMETHING TO MAKE THE GIANT SNEEZE.
AHHHHHH
CHOO!
HA!
THANKS!

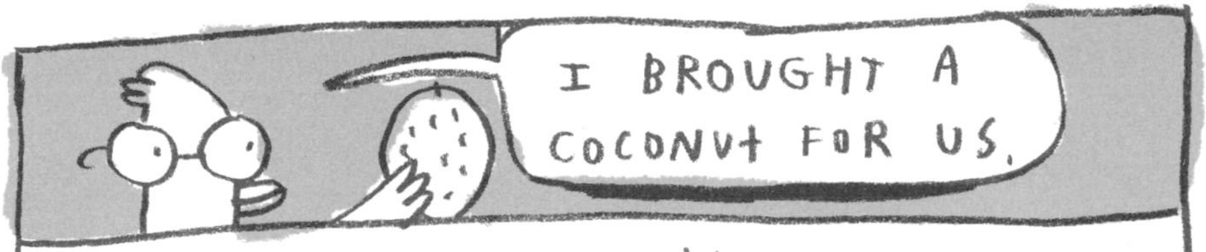
I BROUGHT A COCONUT FOR US.

DRAW SOMEthing to CHOP IT IN HALF.

↓

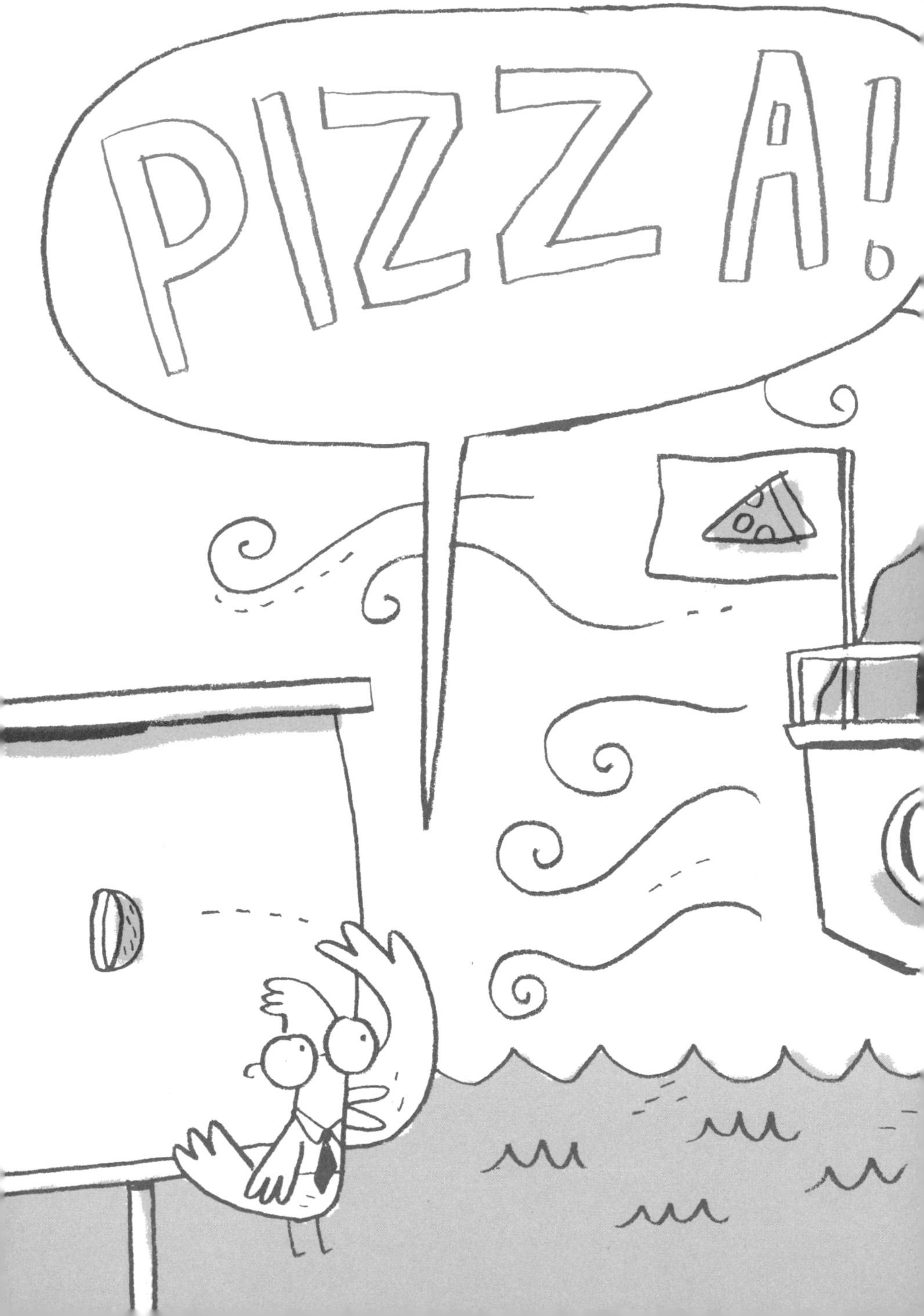
PIZZA!

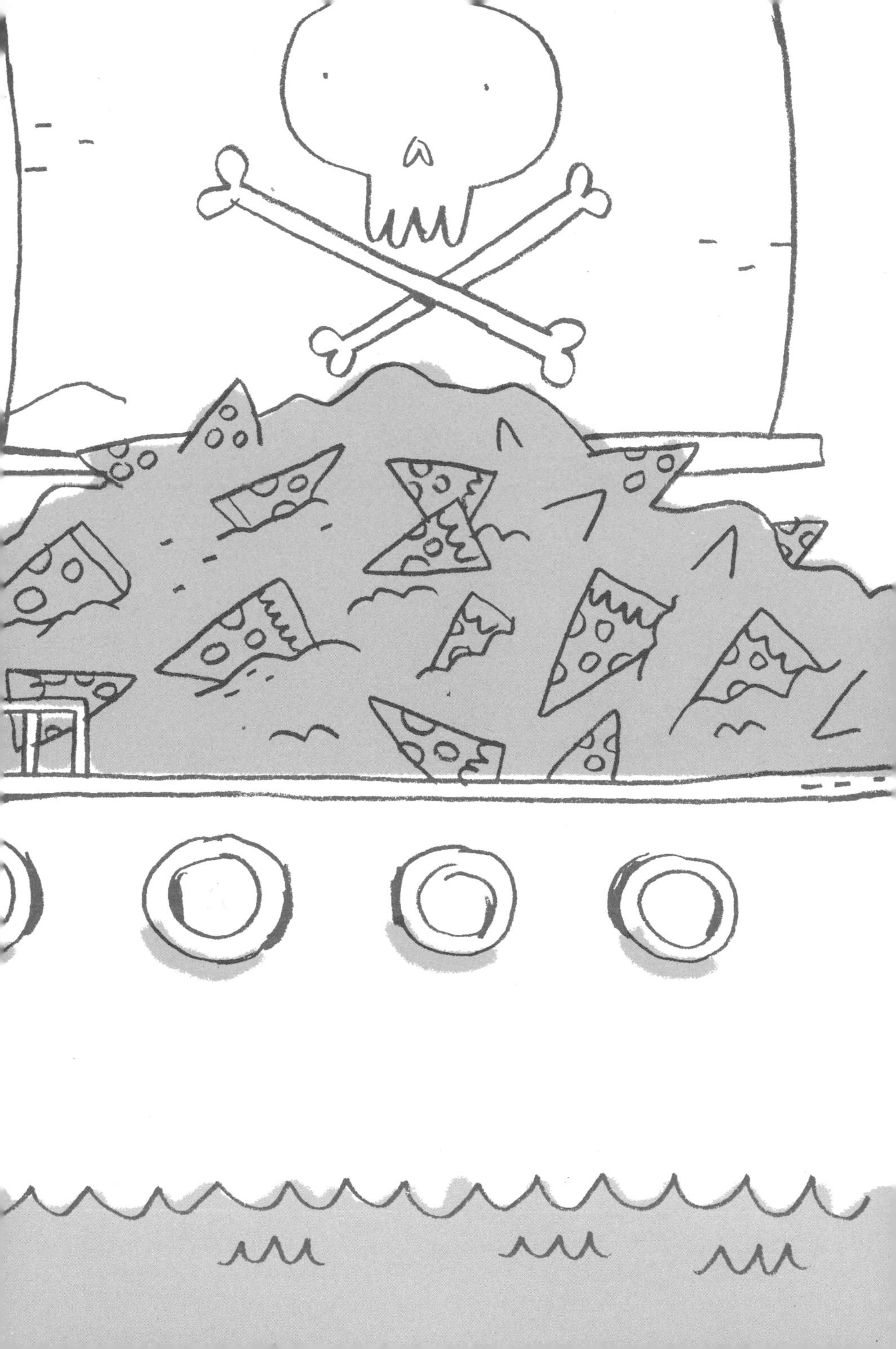

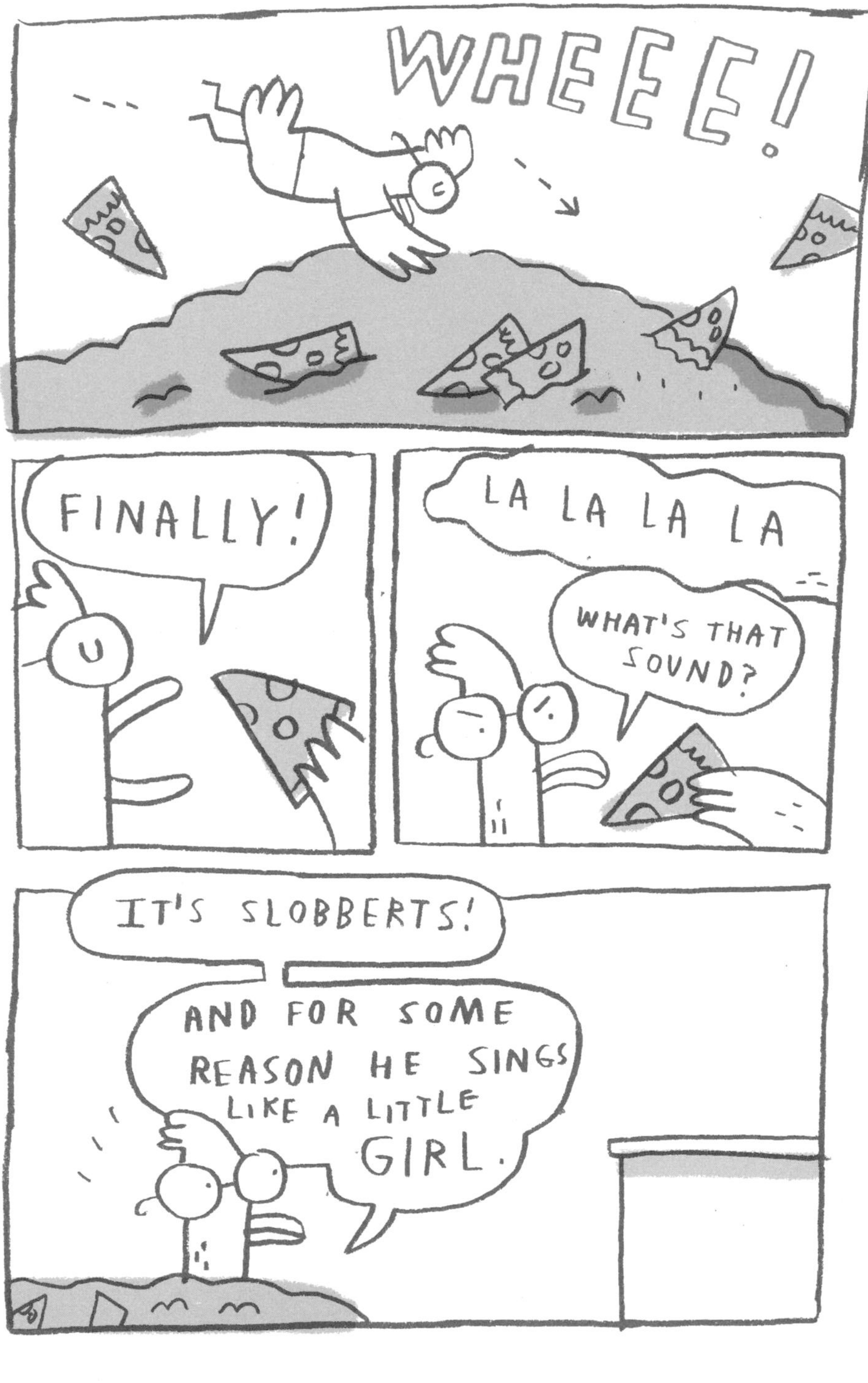
WHEEE!
FINALLY!
LA LA LA LA
WHAT'S THAT SOUND?
IT'S SLOBBERTS!
AND FOR SOME REASON HE SINGS LIKE A LITTLE GIRL.

QUICK! DRAW SOMETHING TO TRAP SLOBBERTS.

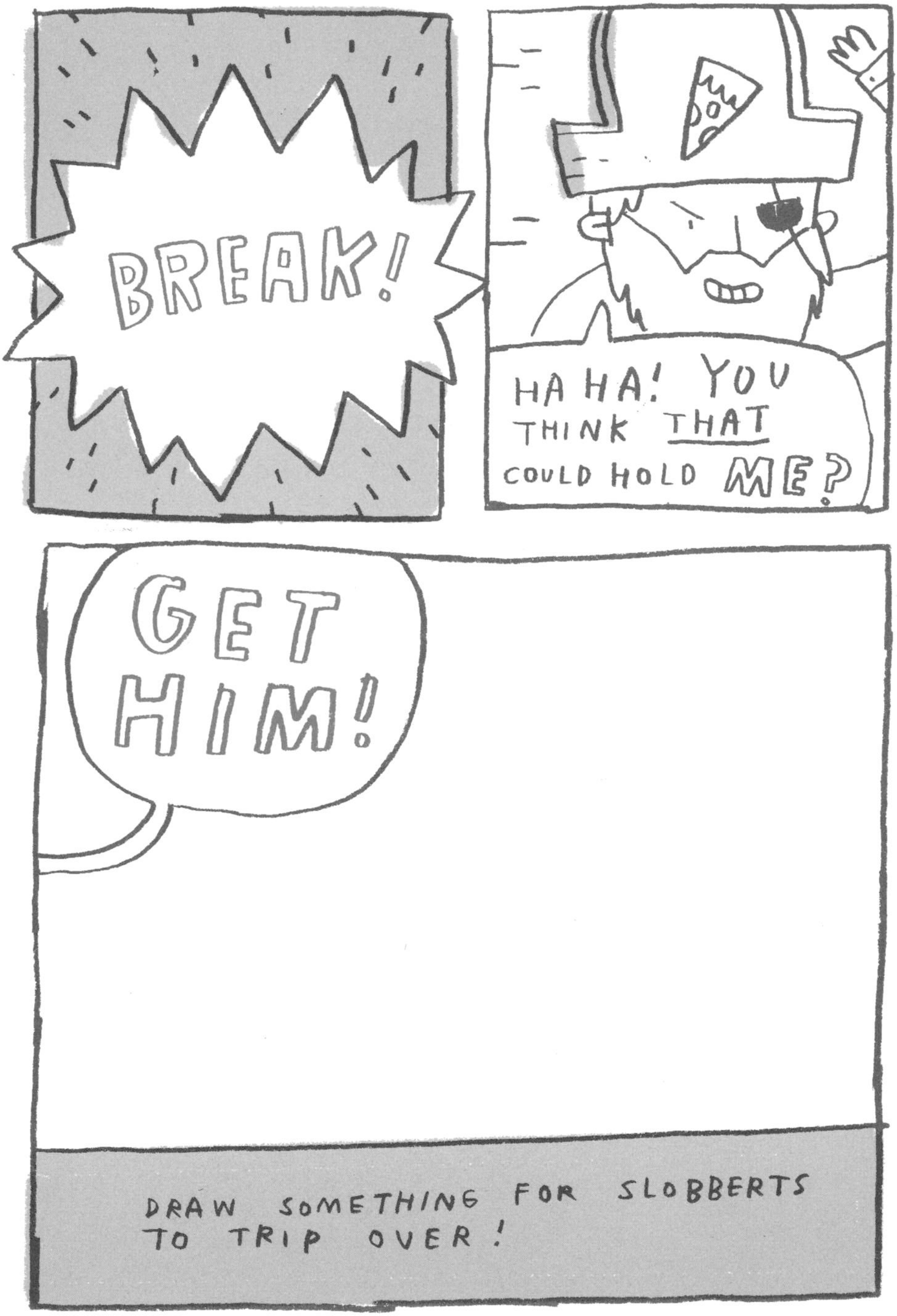
BREAK!
HA HA! YOU THINK THAT COULD HOLD ME?
GET HIM!
DRAW SOMETHING FOR SLOBBERTS TO TRIP OVER!

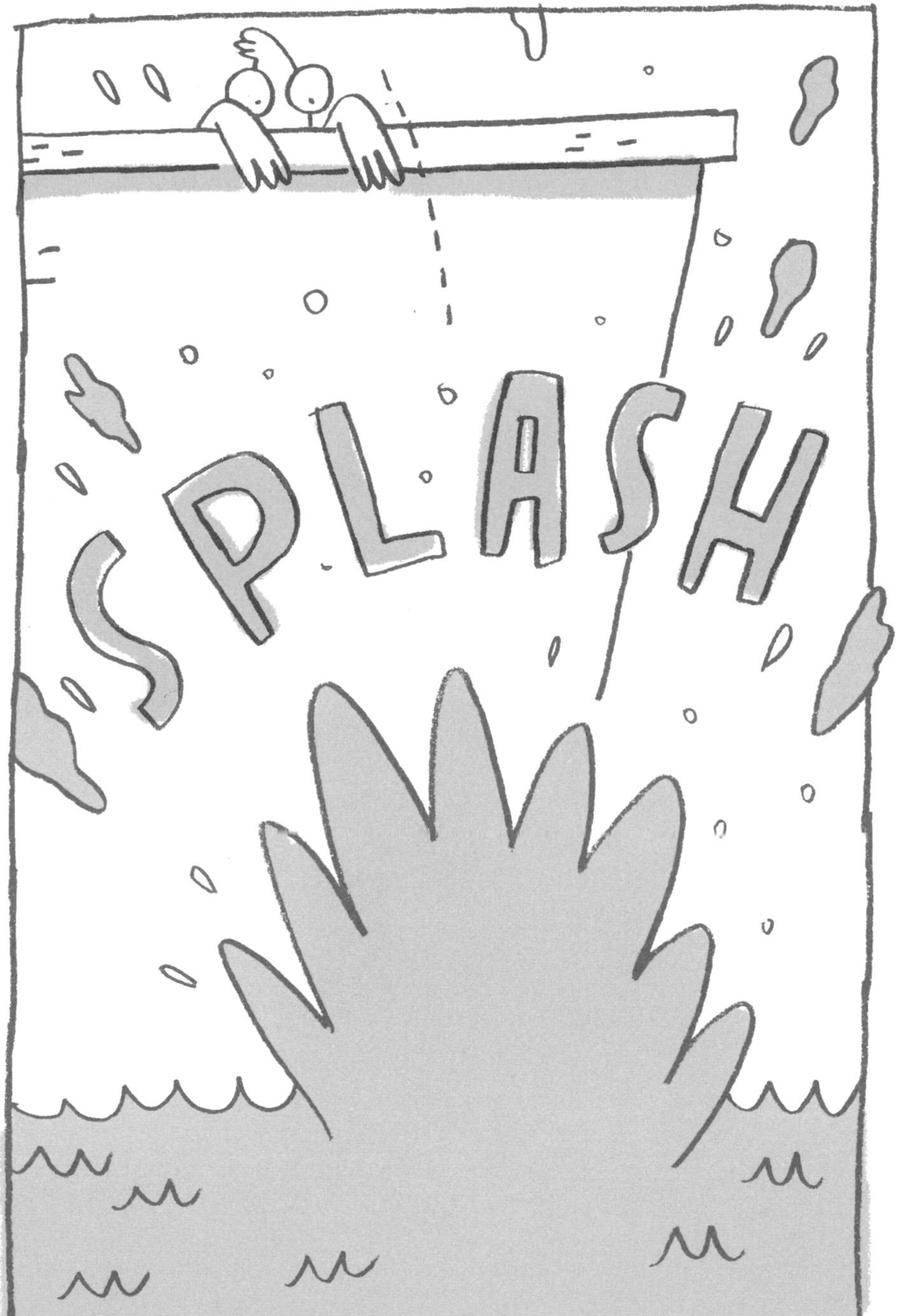
SPLASH

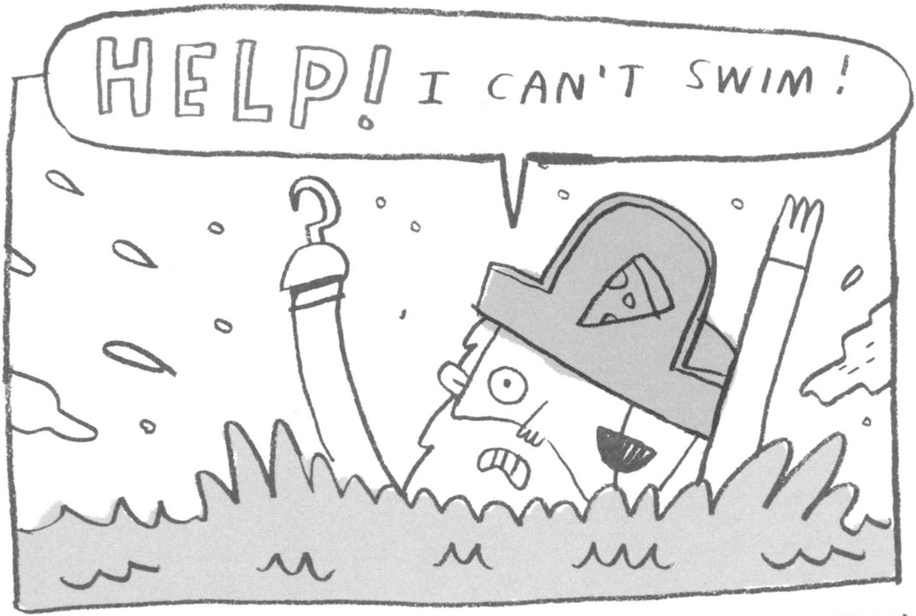
HELP! I CAN'T SWIM!

DRAW SOMETHING FOR SLOBBERTS TO USE TO FLOAT ON.

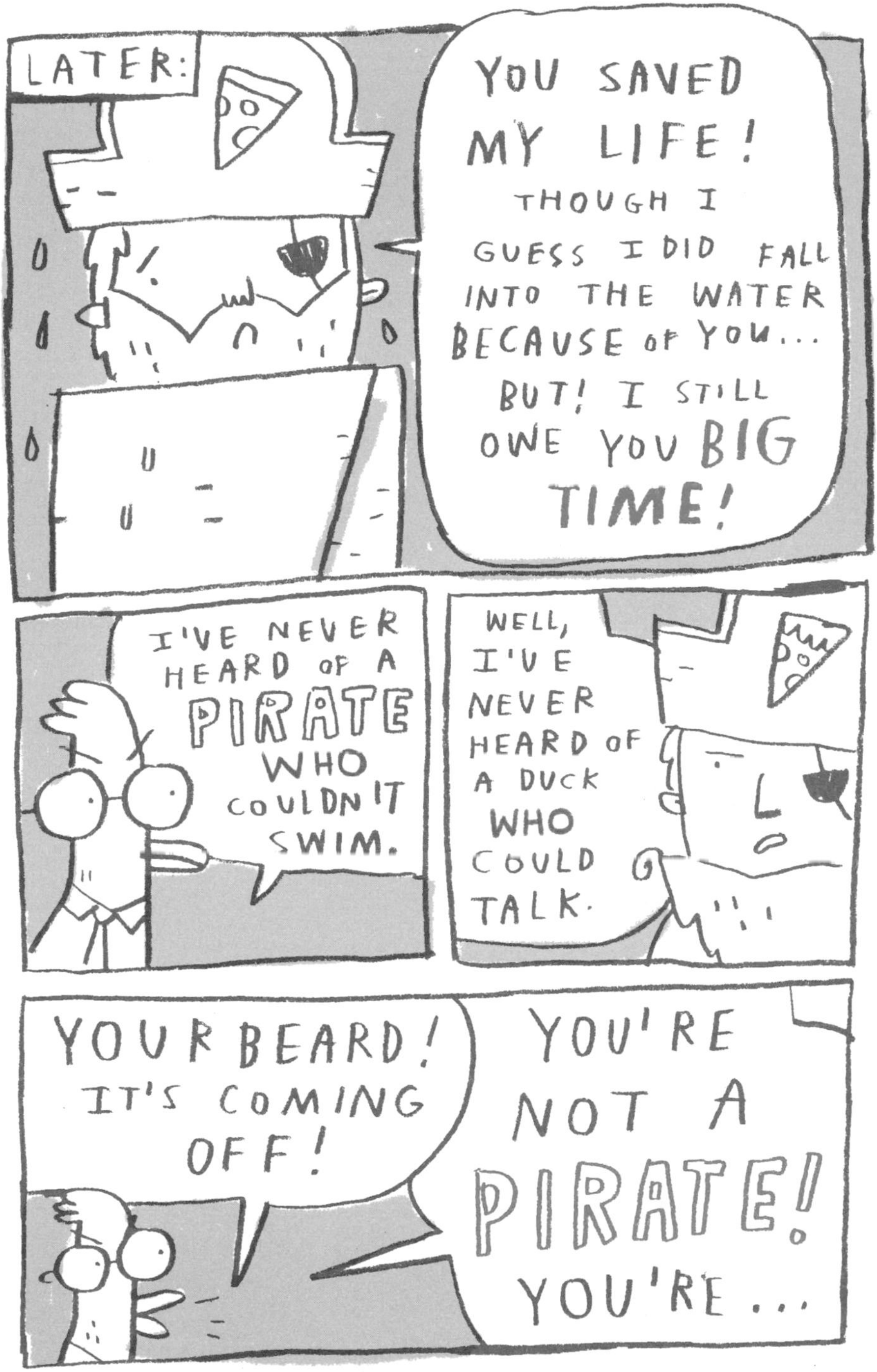
LATER:
YOU SAVED MY LIFE! THOUGH I GUESS I DID FALL INTO THE WATER BECAUSE OF YOU... BUT! I STILL OWE YOU BIG TIME!
I'VE NEVER HEARD OF A PIRATE WHO COULDN'T SWIM.
WELL, I'VE NEVER HEARD OF A DUCK WHO COULD TALK.
YOUR BEARD! IT'S COMING OFF!
YOU'RE NOT A PIRATE! YOU'RE...

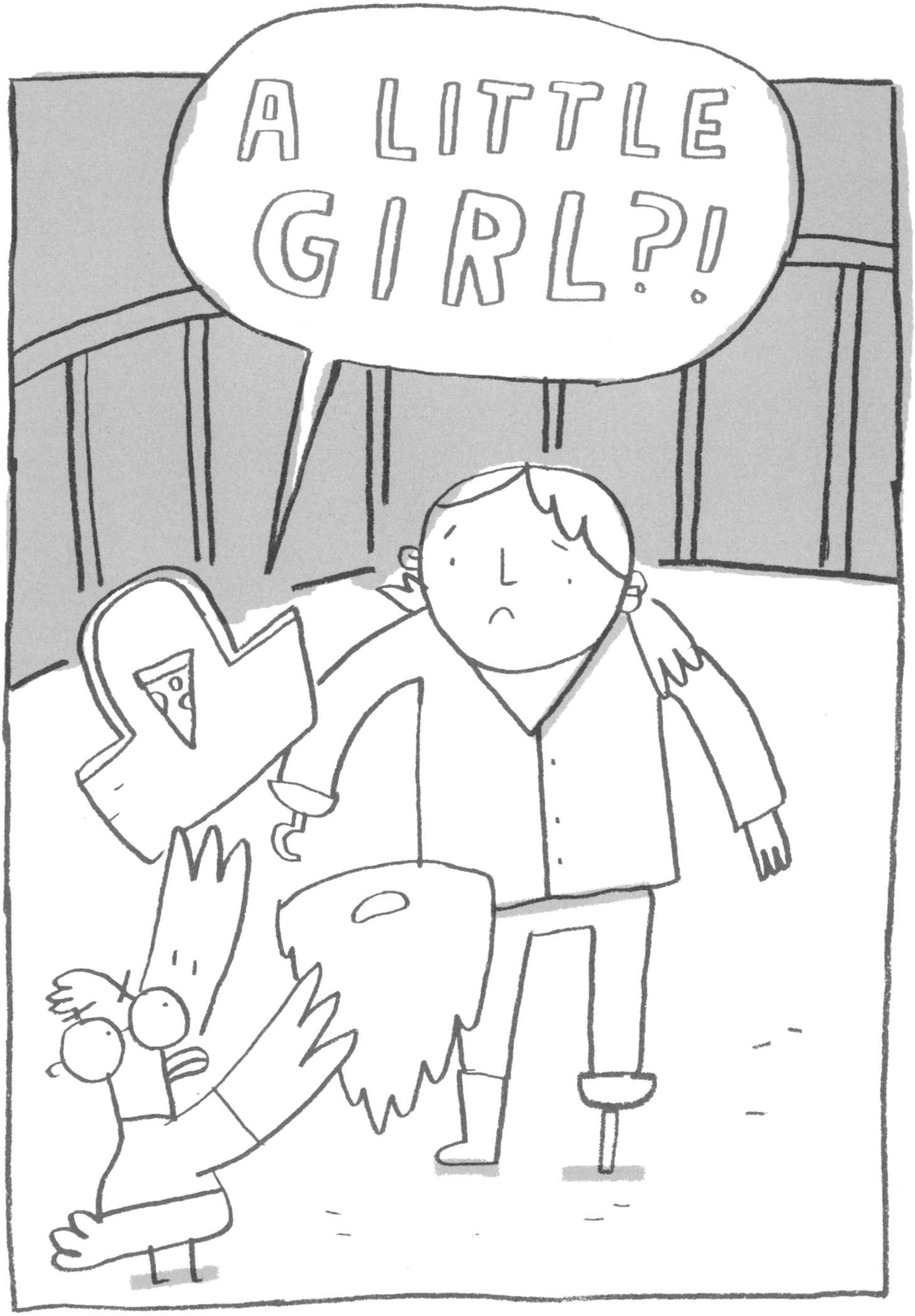
A LITTLE GIRL?!

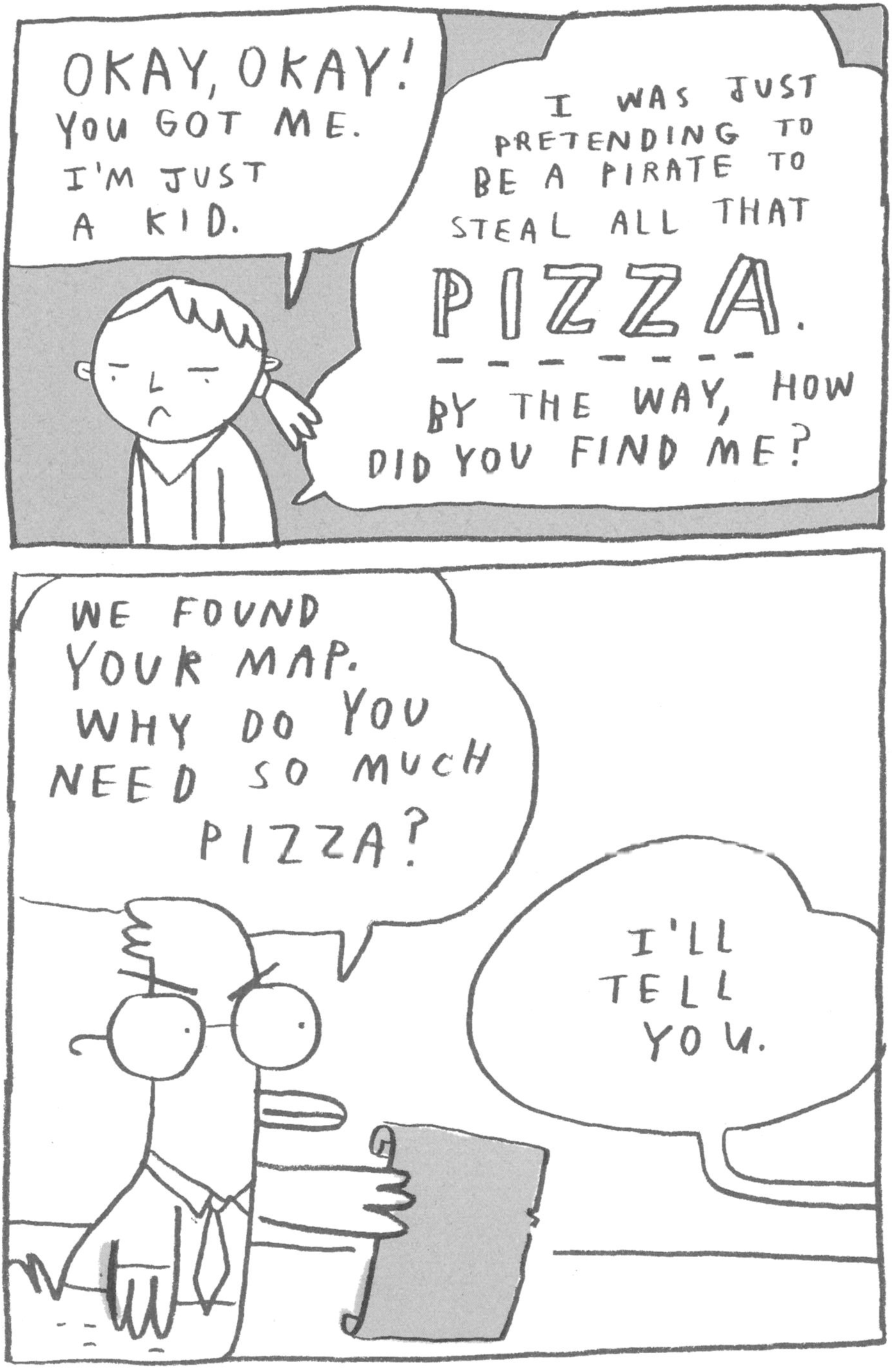
OKAY, OKAY! YOU GOT ME. I'M JUST A KID.
I WAS JUST PRETENDING TO BE A PIRATE TO STEAL ALL THAT PIZZA.
BY THE WAY, HOW DID YOU FIND ME?
WE FOUND YOUR MAP. WHY DO YOU NEED SO MUCH PIZZA?
I'LL TELL YOU.

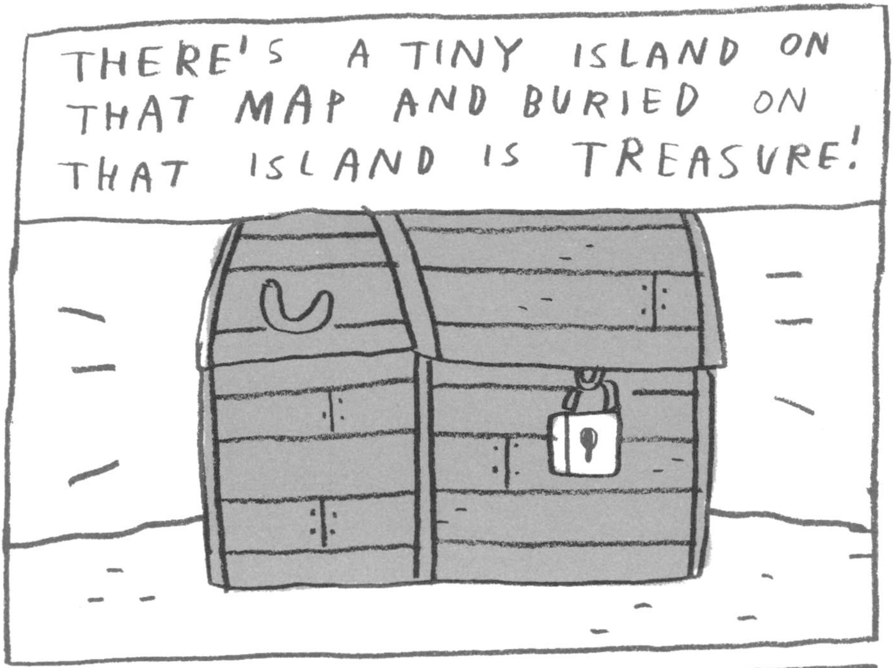
THERE'S A TINY ISLAND ON THAT MAP AND BURIED ON THAT ISLAND IS TREASURE!

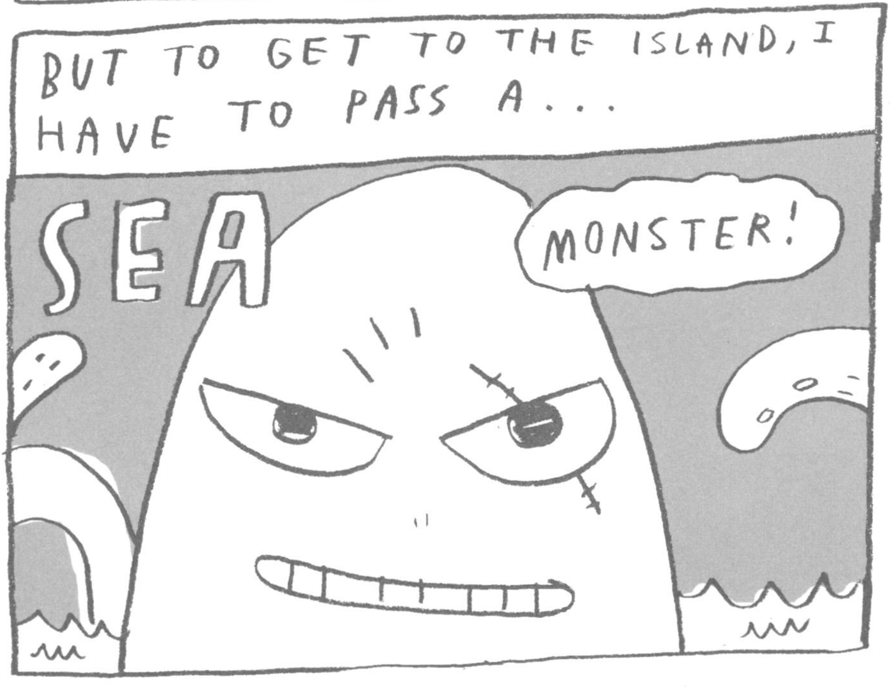
BUT TO GET TO THE ISLAND, I HAVE TO PASS A...
SEA
MONSTER!

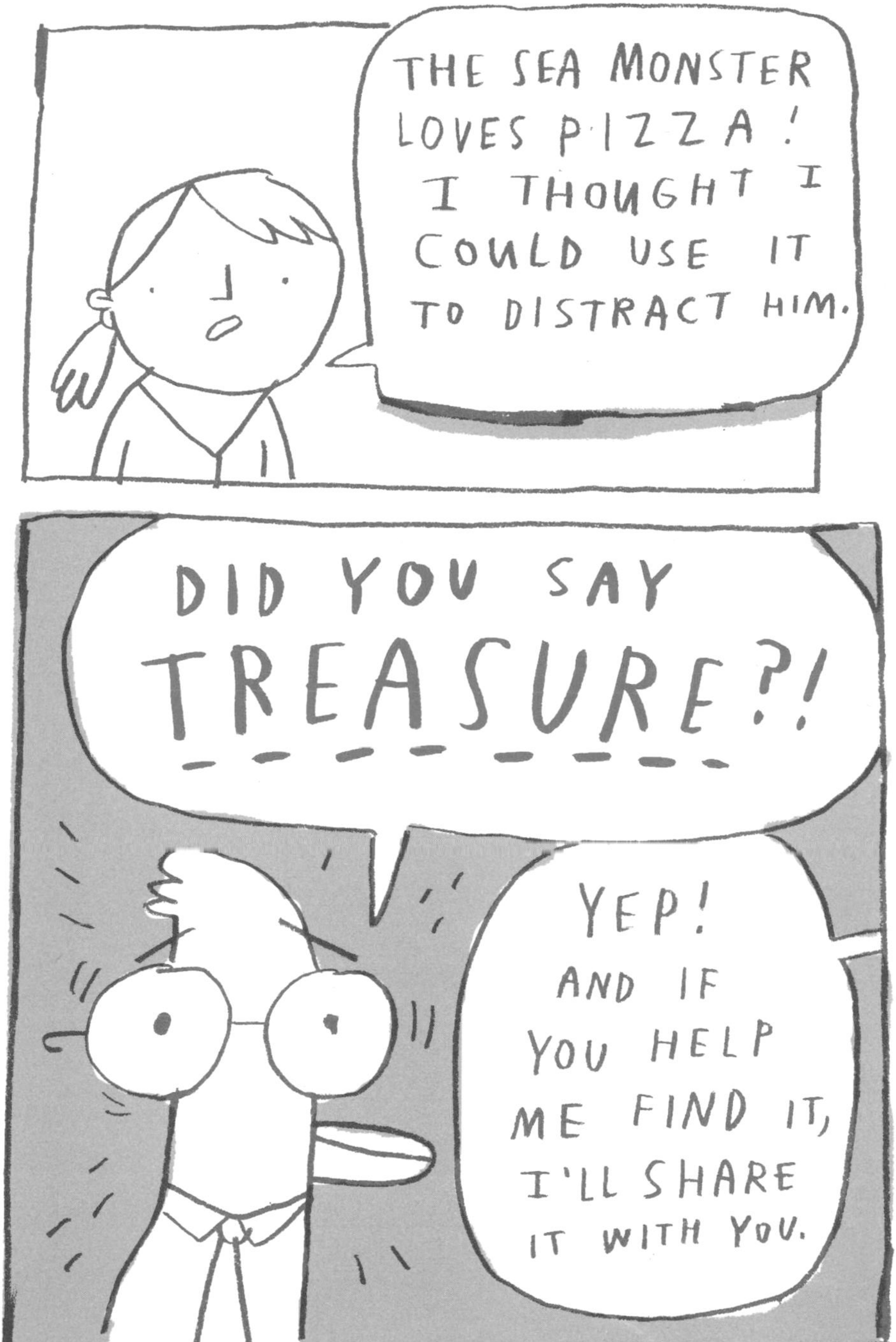
THE SEA MONSTER LOVES PIZZA! I THOUGHT I COULD USE IT TO DISTRACT HIM.
DID YOU SAY TREASURE?!
YEP! AND IF YOU HELP ME FIND IT, I'LL SHARE IT WITH YOU.

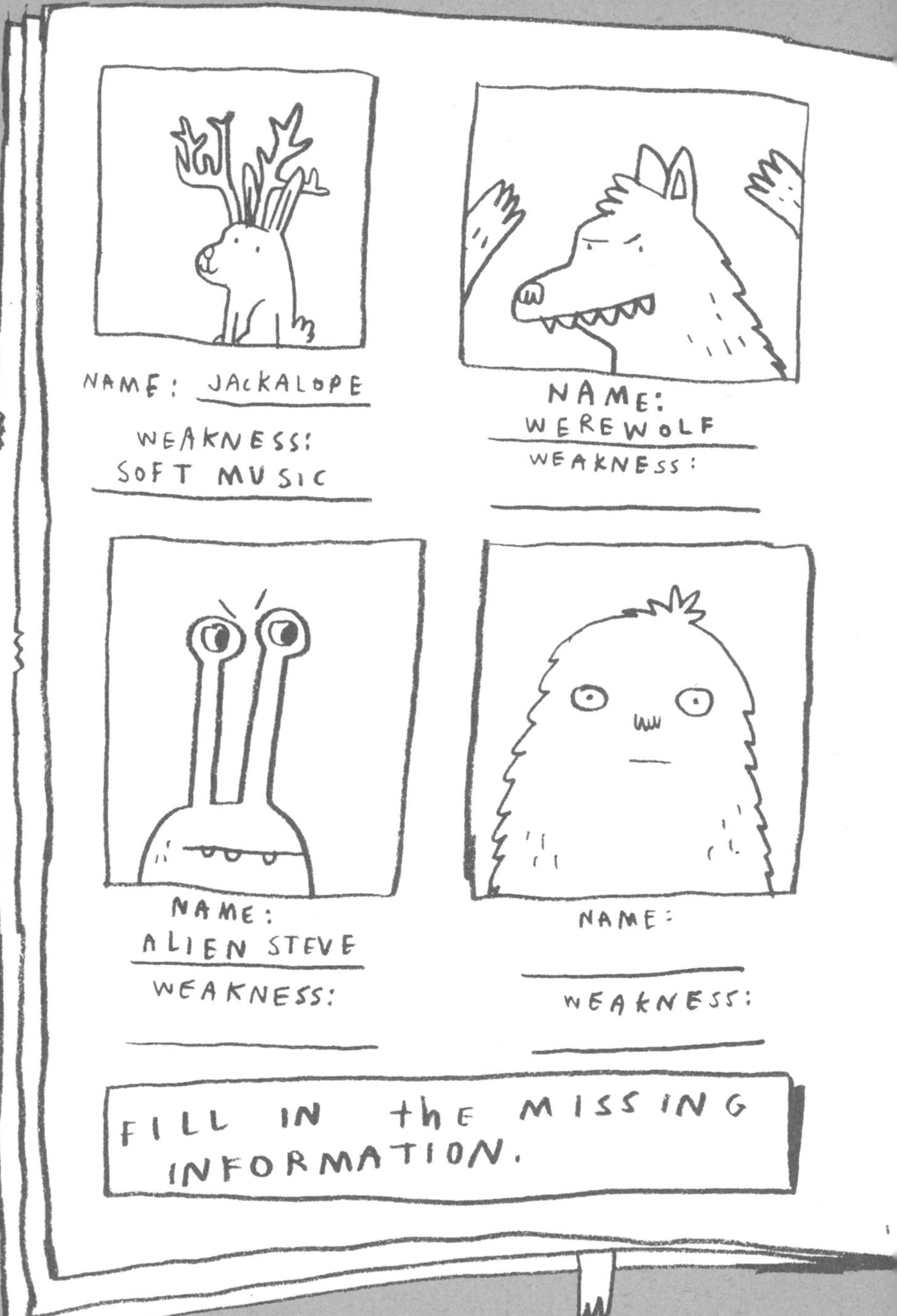
NAME: JACKALOPE
WEAKNESS: SOFT MUSIC
NAME: WEREWOLF
WEAKNESS:
NAME: ALIEN STEVE
WEAKNESS:
NAME:
WEAKNESS:
FILL IN the MISSING INFORMATION.

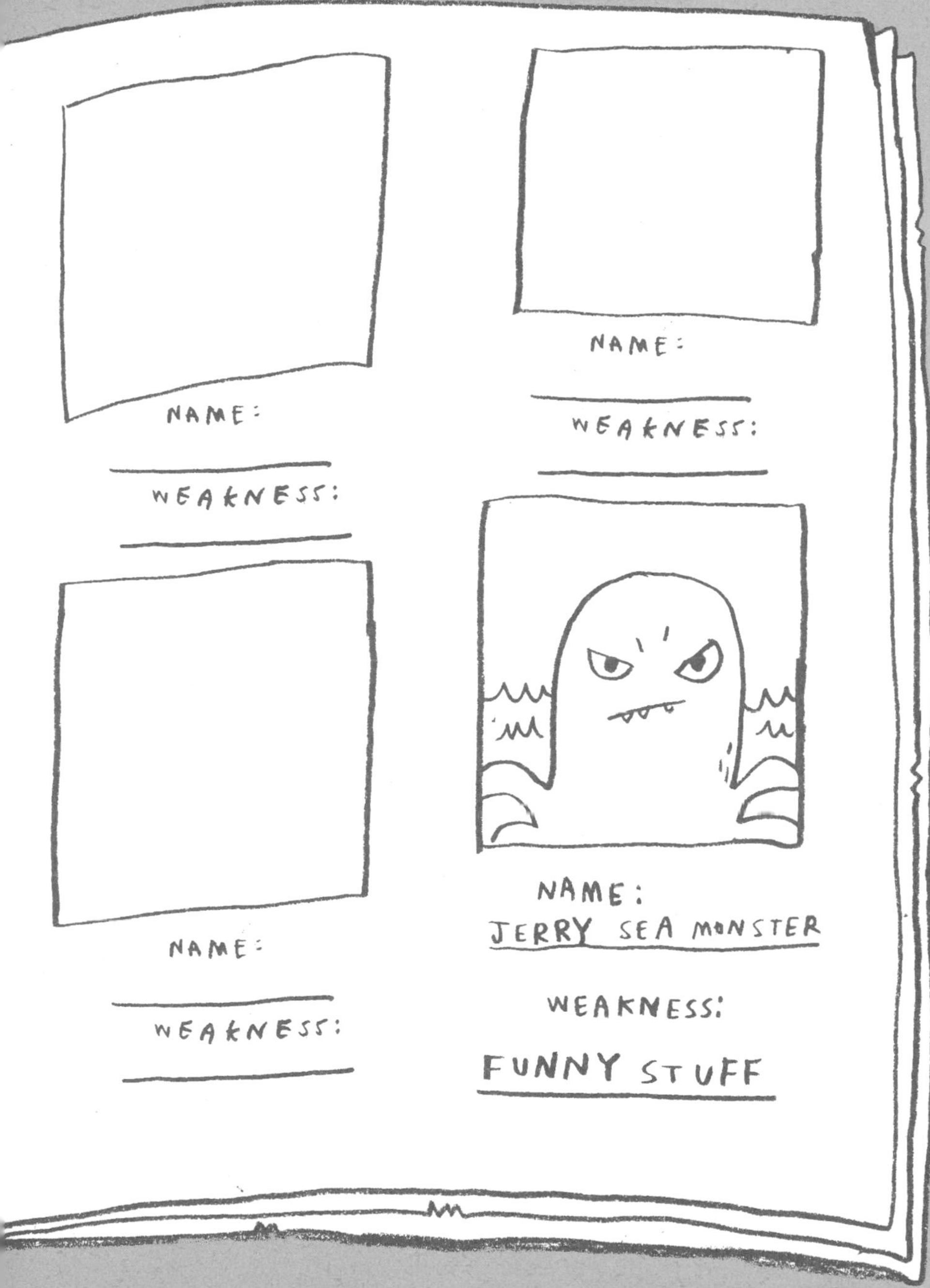
NAME:
WEAKNESS:
NAME:
WEAKNESS:
NAME:
WEAKNESS:
NAME:
JERRY SEA MONSTER
WEAKNESS:
FUNNY STUFF

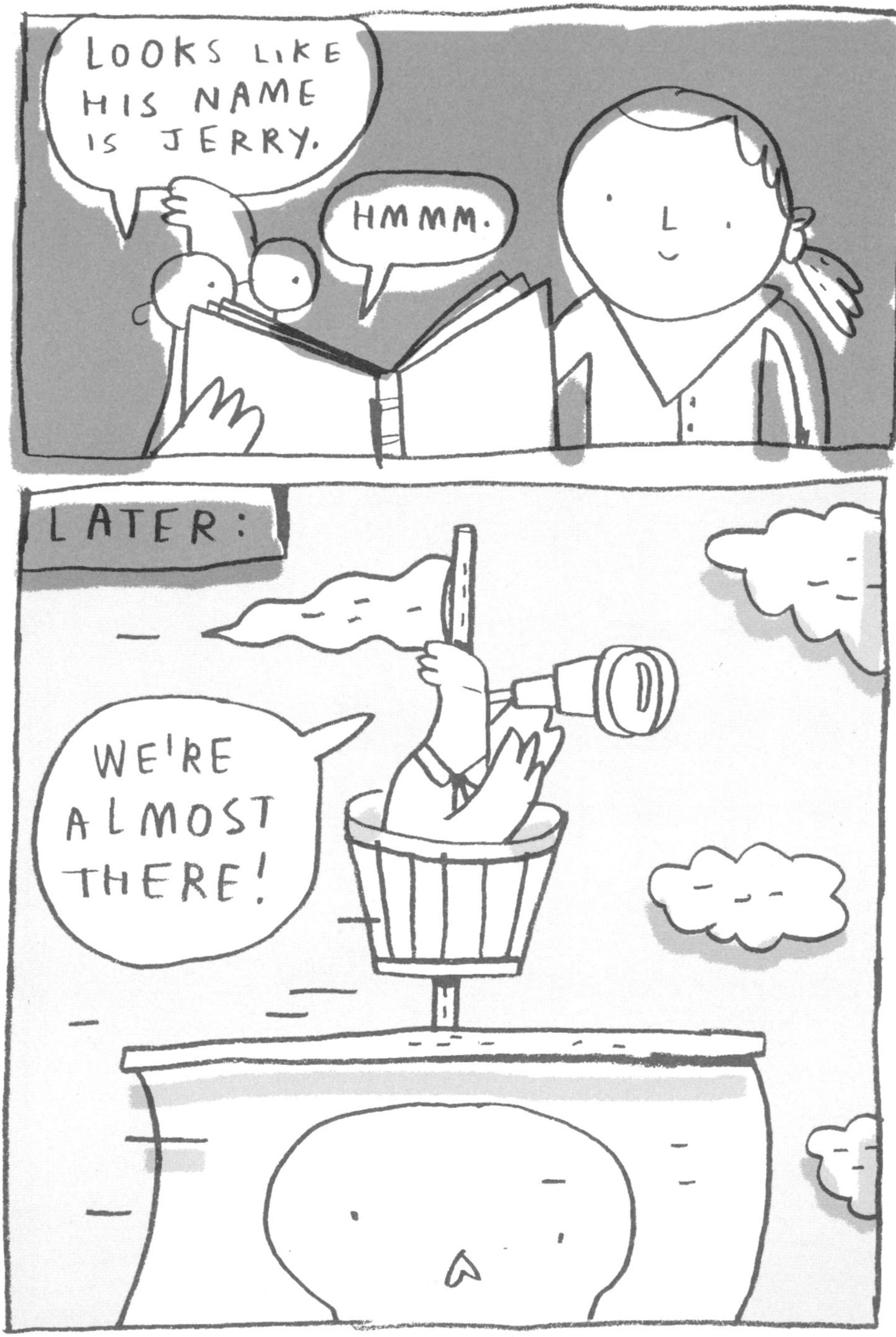
LOOKS LIKE HIS NAME IS JERRY.
HMMM.
LATER:
WE'RE ALMOST THERE!

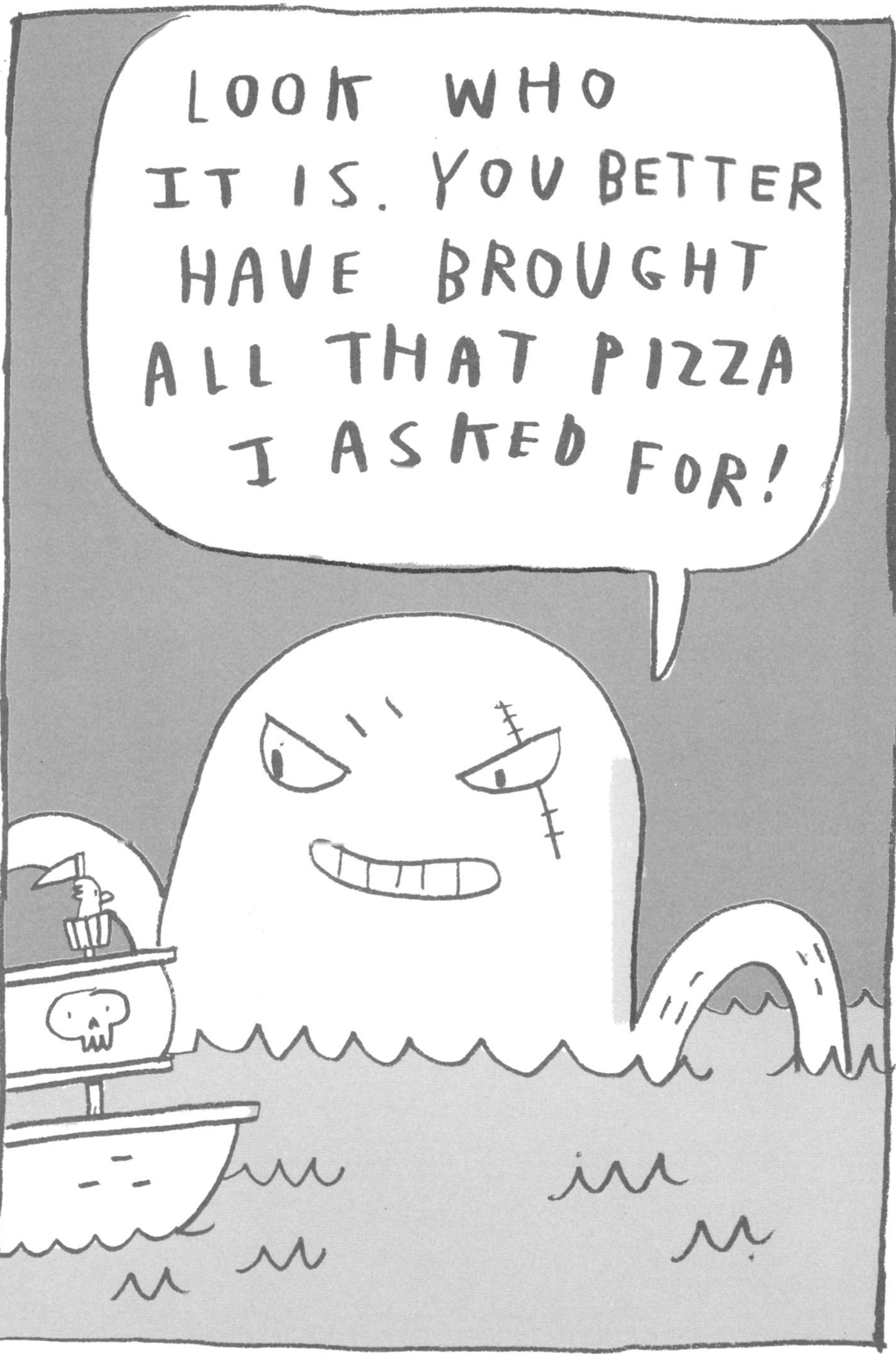
LOOK WHO IT IS. YOU BETTER HAVE BROUGHT ALL THAT PIZZA I ASKED FOR!

DRAW SOMETHING SUPER DUPER

FUNNY

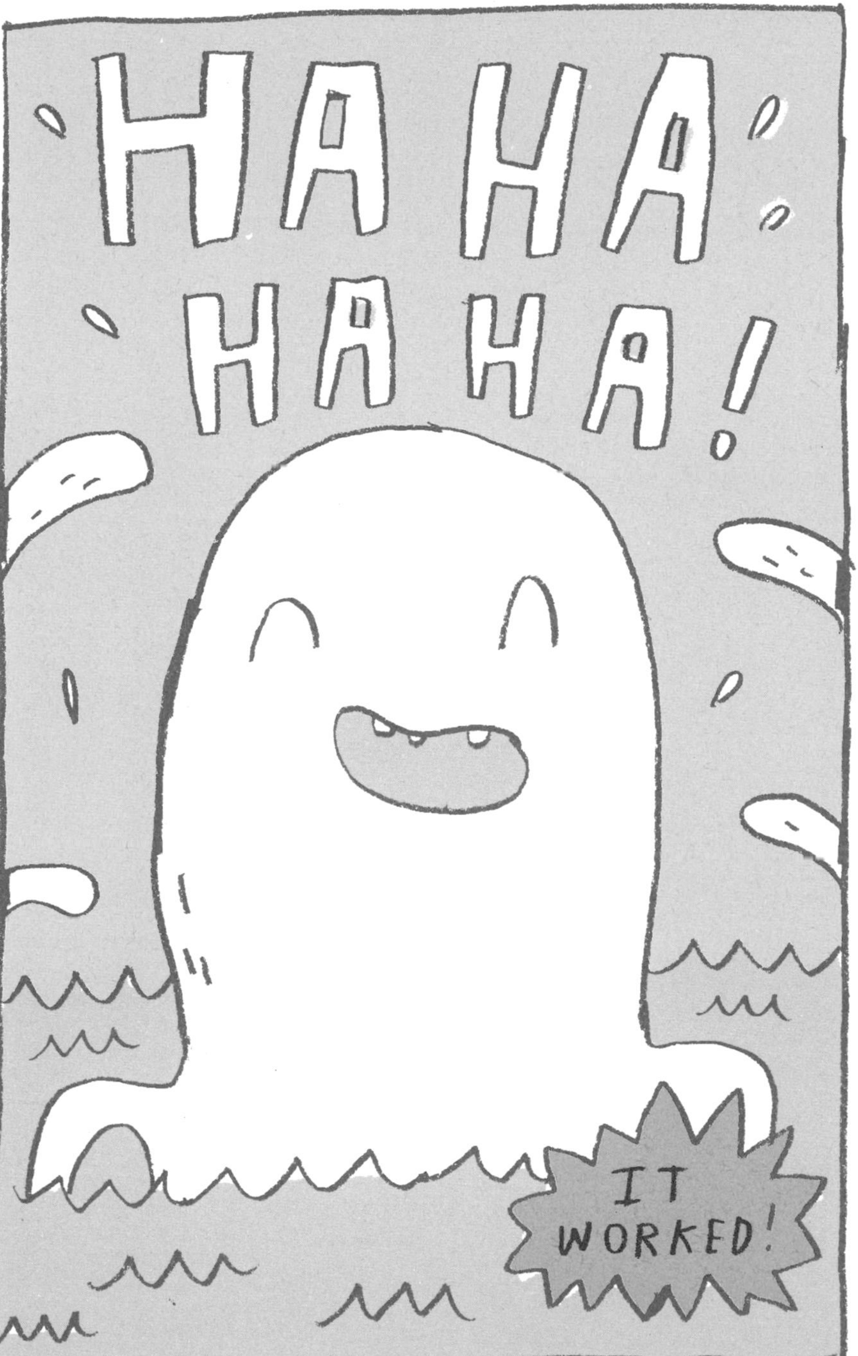
HA HA HA HA
HA HA HA HA!
IT WORKED!

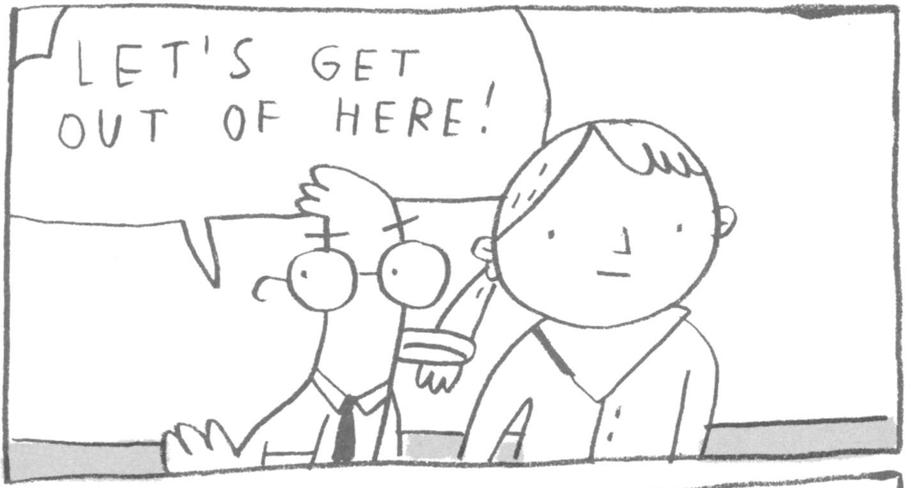
LET'S GET OUT OF HERE!

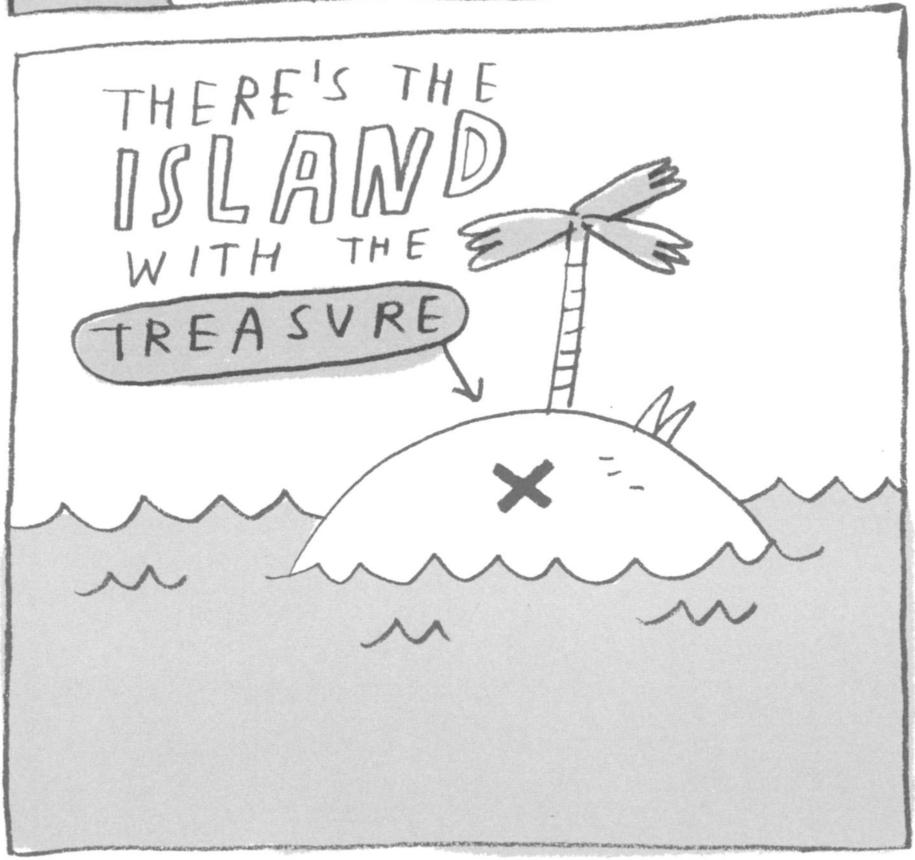
THERE'S THE ISLAND WITH THE
TREASURE

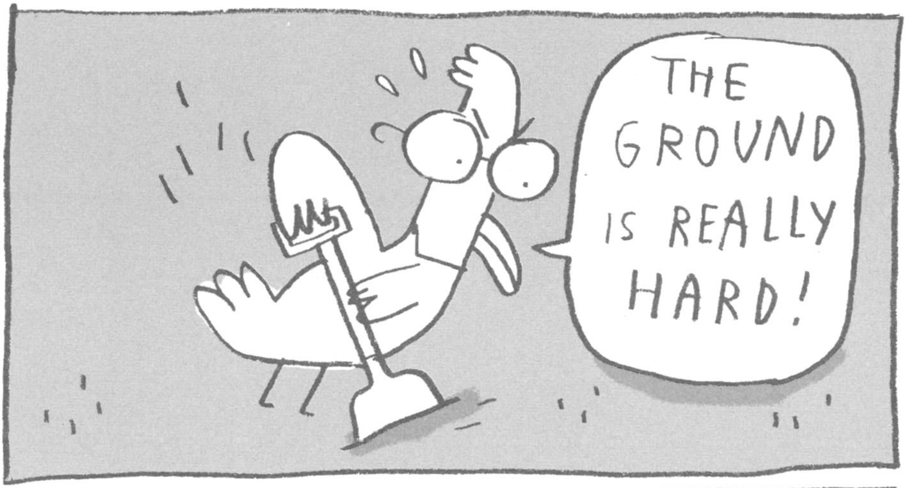
THE GROUND IS REALLY HARD!

DRAW AN AWESOME DIGGING MACHINE.

THE TREASURE!!

IT'S LOCKED!

DRAW SOMETHING TO OPEN THE TREASURE CHEST.

IT DIDN'T WORK! TRY DRAWING SOMETHING REALLY HEAVY TO SMASH IT OPEN!

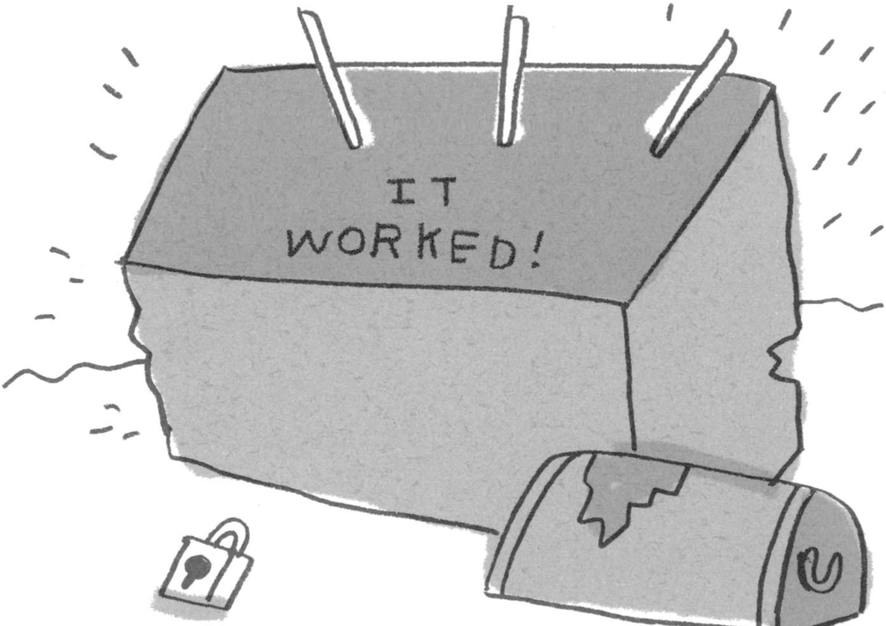
IT WORKED!

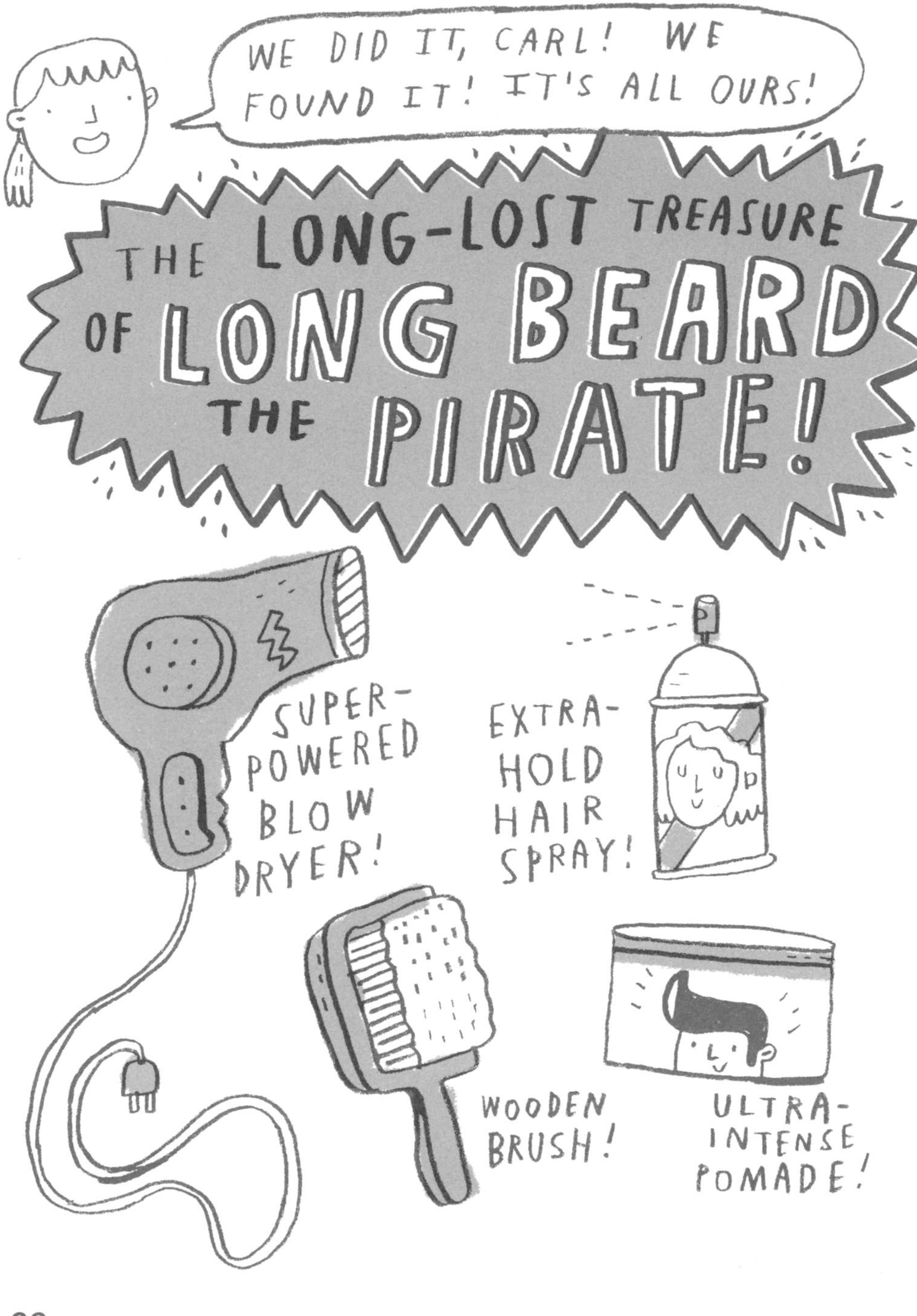
WE DID IT, CARL! WE FOUND IT! IT'S ALL OURS!
THE LONG-LOST TREASURE OF LONG BEARD THE PIRATE!
SUPER-POWERED BLOW DRYER!
EXTRA-HOLD HAIR SPRAY!
WOODEN BRUSH!
ULTRA-INTENSE POMADE!

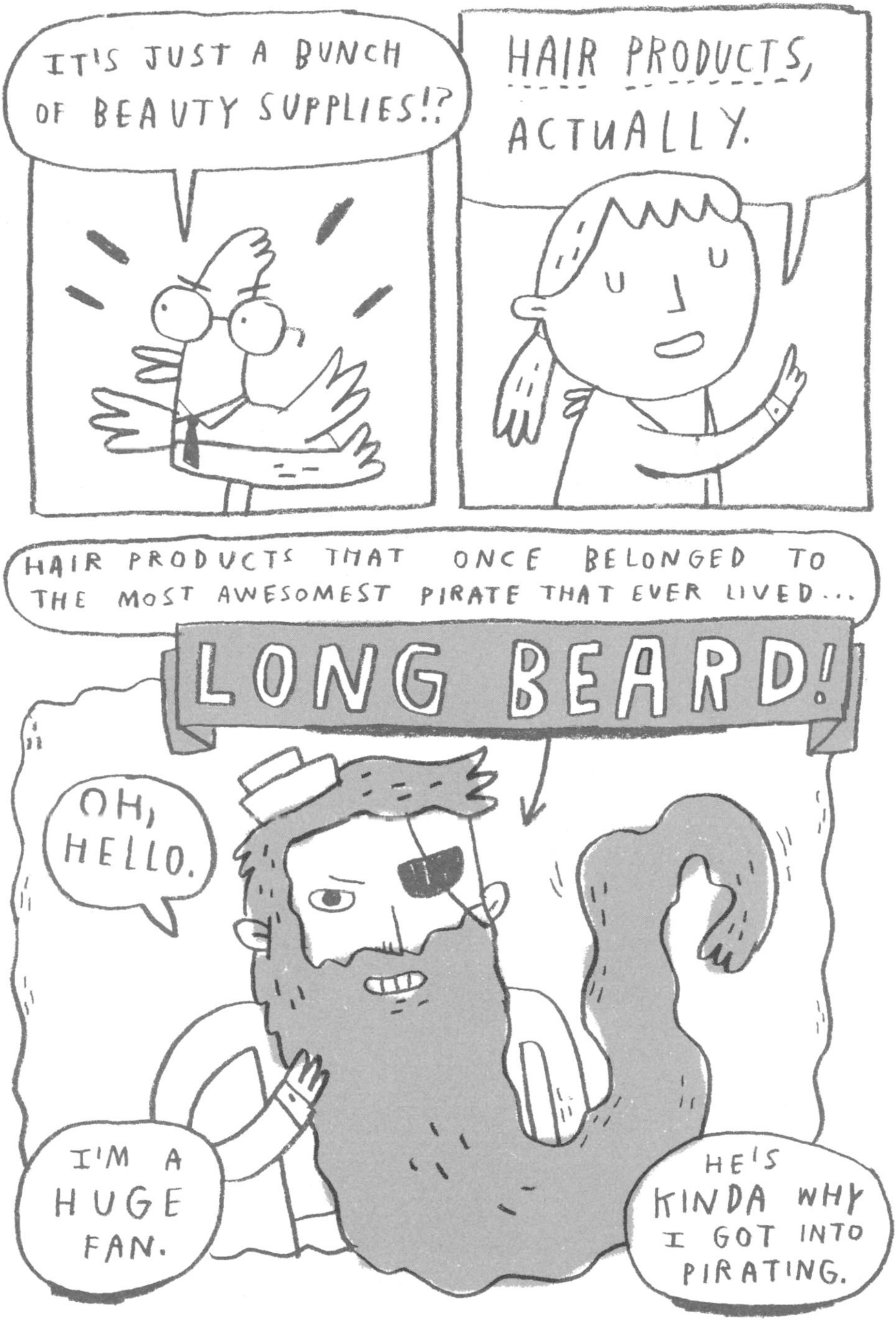
IT'S JUST A BUNCH OF BEAUTY SUPPLIES!?
HAIR PRODUCTS, ACTUALLY.
HAIR PRODUCTS THAT ONCE BELONGED TO THE MOST AWESOMEST PIRATE THAT EVER LIVED...
LONG BEARD!
OH, HELLO.
I'M A HUGE FAN.
HE'S KINDA WHY I GOT INTO PIRATING.

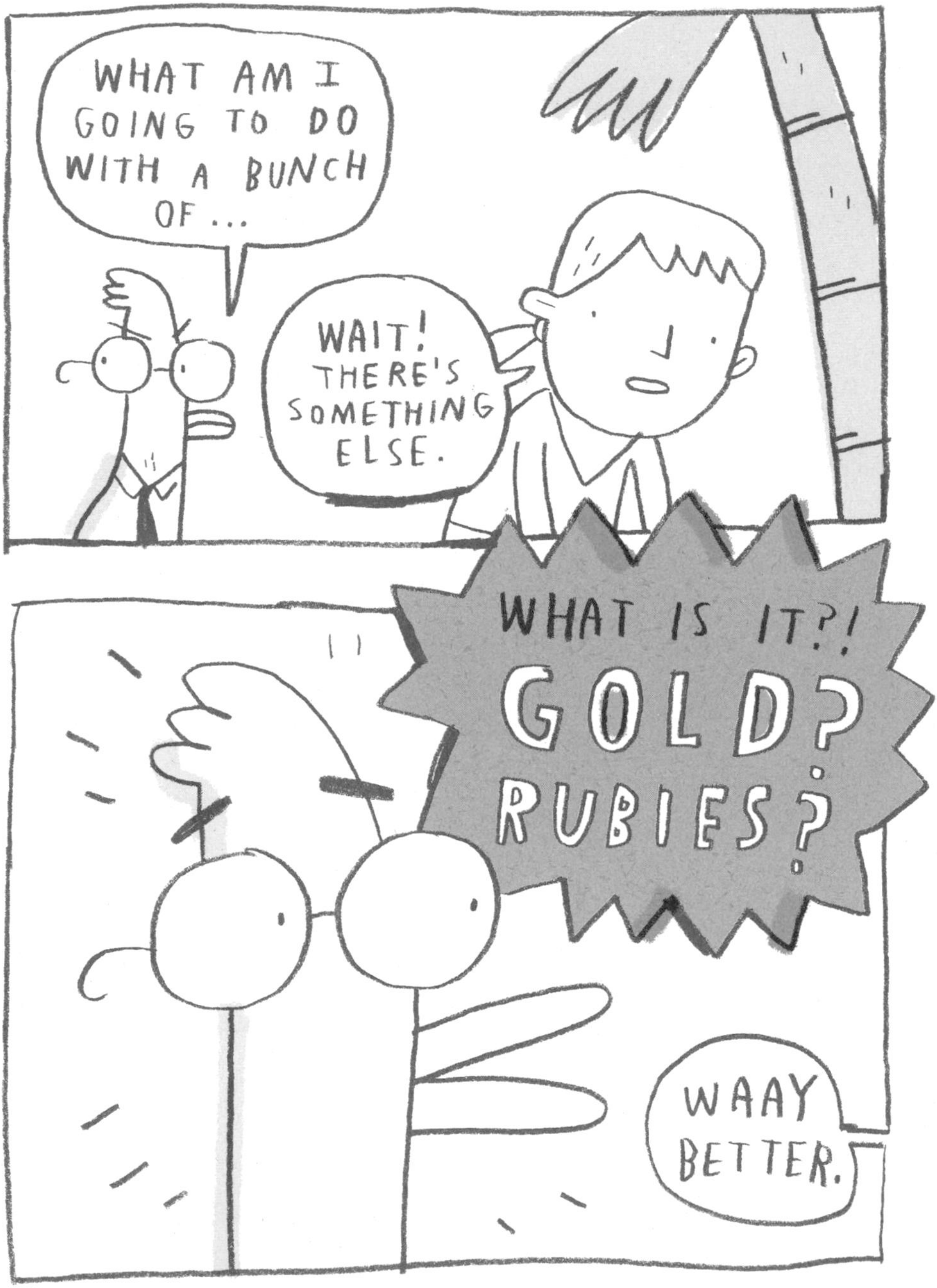
WHAT AM I GOING TO DO WITH A BUNCH OF ...
WAIT! THERE'S SOMETHING ELSE.
WHAT IS IT?! GOLD? RUBIES?
WAAY BETTER.

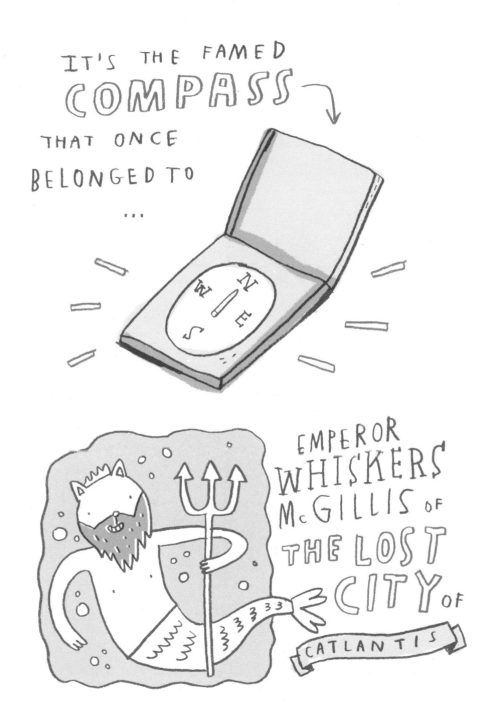

IT'S THE FAMED

COMPASS

THAT ONCE

BELONGED TO

...

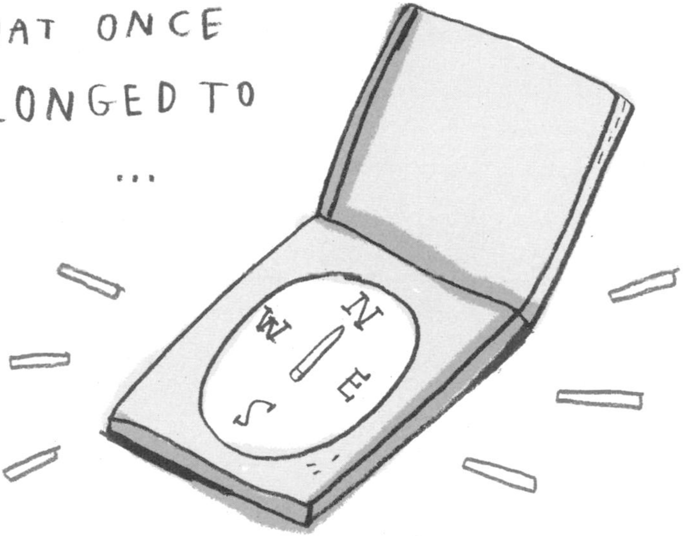
N
W
E
S

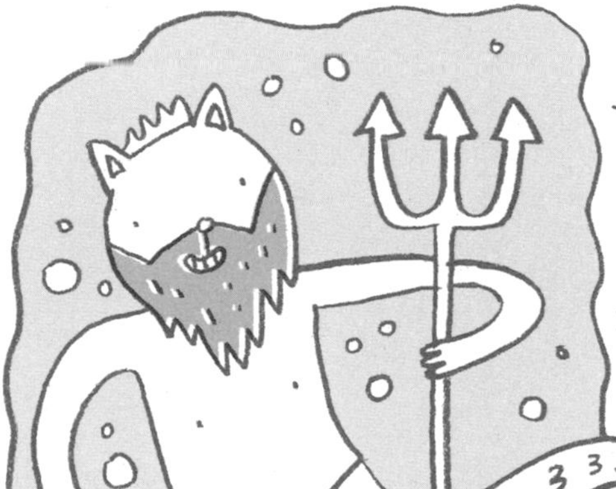

EMPEROR WHISKERS McGILLIS OF THE LOST CITY OF CATLANTIS

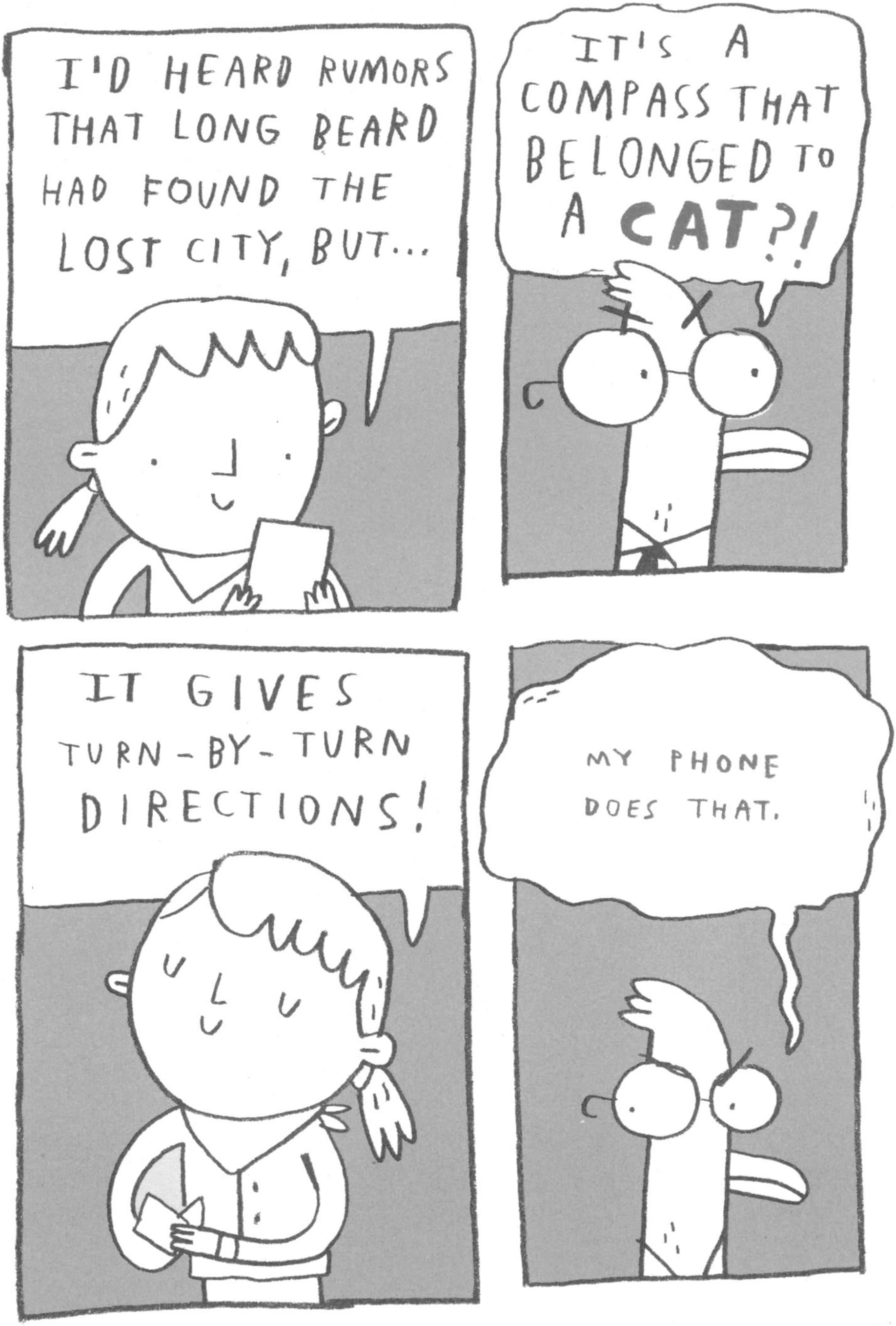
I'D HEARD RUMORS THAT LONG BEARD HAD FOUND THE LOST CITY, BUT...
IT'S A COMPASS THAT BELONGED TO A CAT?!
IT GIVES TURN-BY-TURN DIRECTIONS!
MY PHONE DOES THAT.

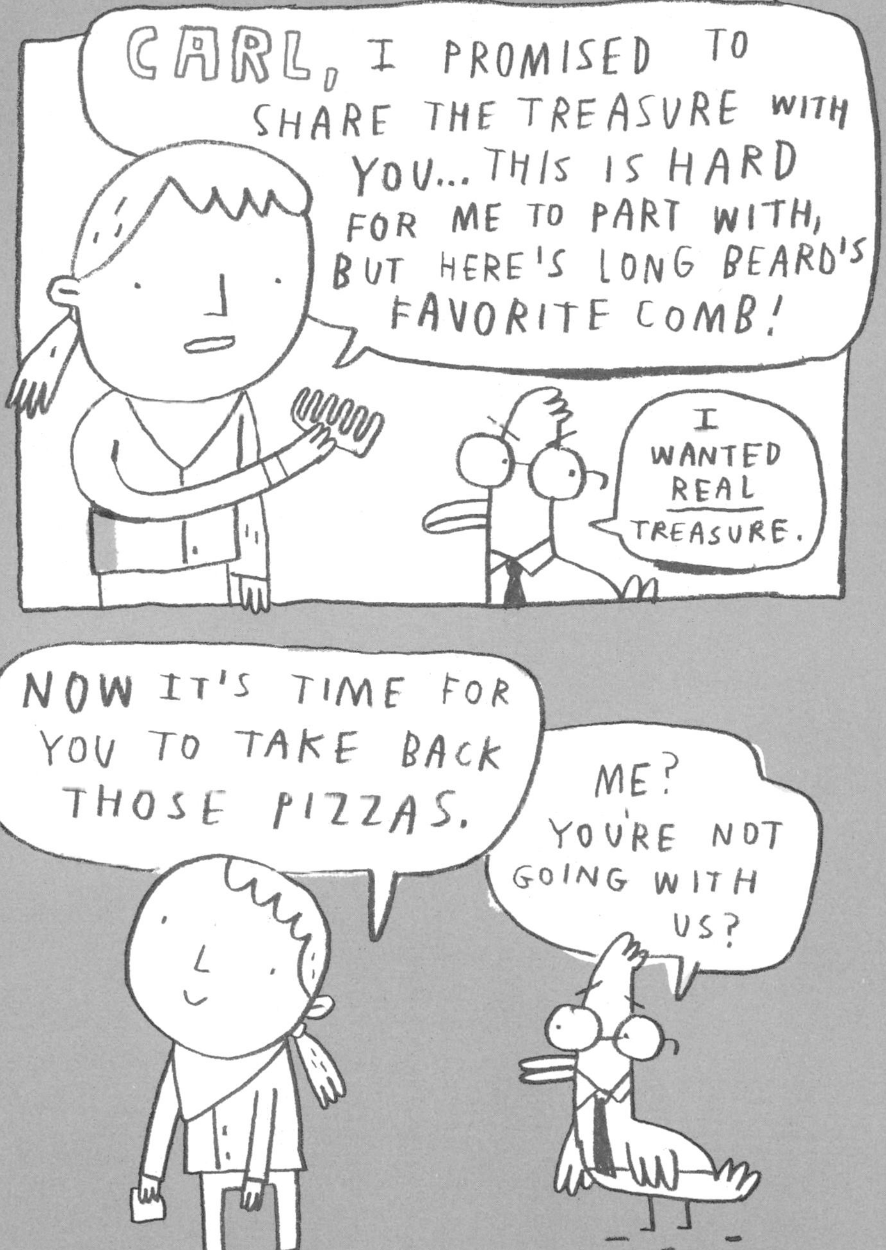
CARL, I PROMISED TO SHARE THE TREASURE WITH YOU... THIS IS HARD FOR ME TO PART WITH, BUT HERE'S LONG BEARD'S FAVORITE COMB!
I WANTED REAL TREASURE.
NOW IT'S TIME FOR YOU TO TAKE BACK THOSE PIZZAS.
ME? YOU'RE NOT GOING WITH US?

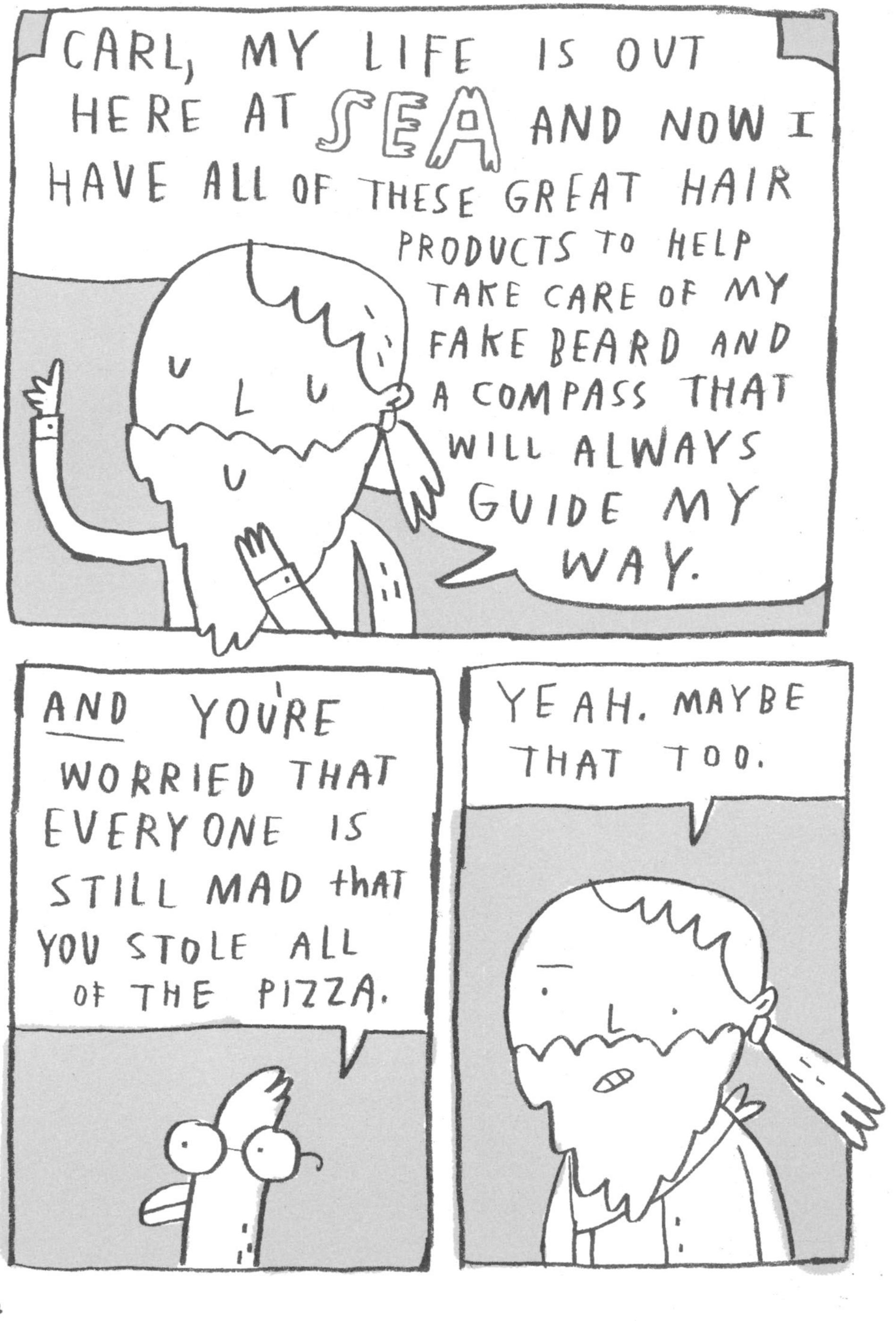
CARL, MY LIFE IS OUT HERE AT SEA AND NOW I HAVE ALL OF THESE GREAT HAIR PRODUCTS TO HELP TAKE CARE OF MY FAKE BEARD AND A COMPASS THAT WILL ALWAYS GUIDE MY WAY.
AND YOU'RE WORRIED THAT EVERYONE IS STILL MAD that YOU STOLE ALL OF THE PIZZA.
YEAH. MAYBE THAT TOO.

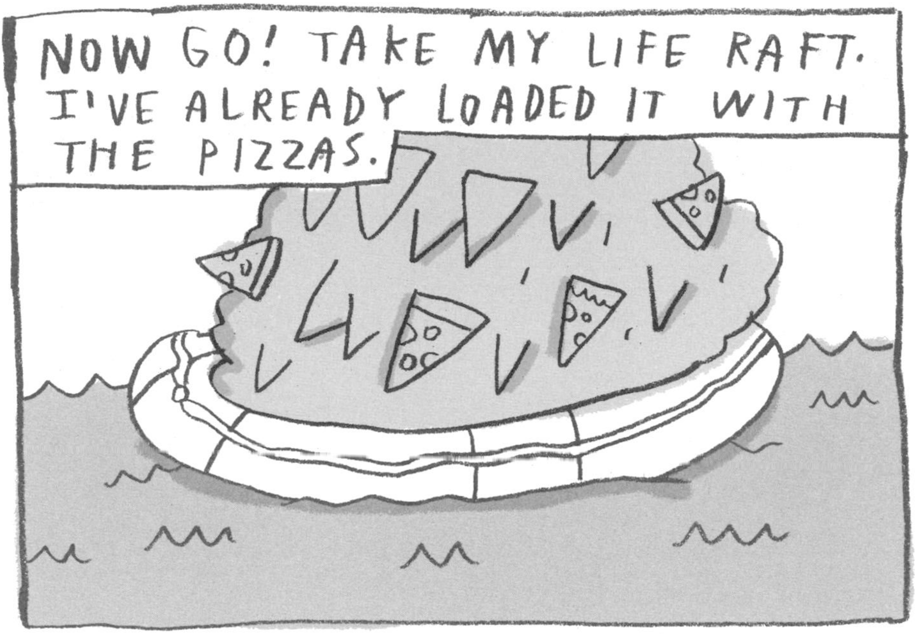
NOW GO! TAKE MY LIFE RAFT. I'VE ALREADY LOADED IT WITH THE PIZZAS.

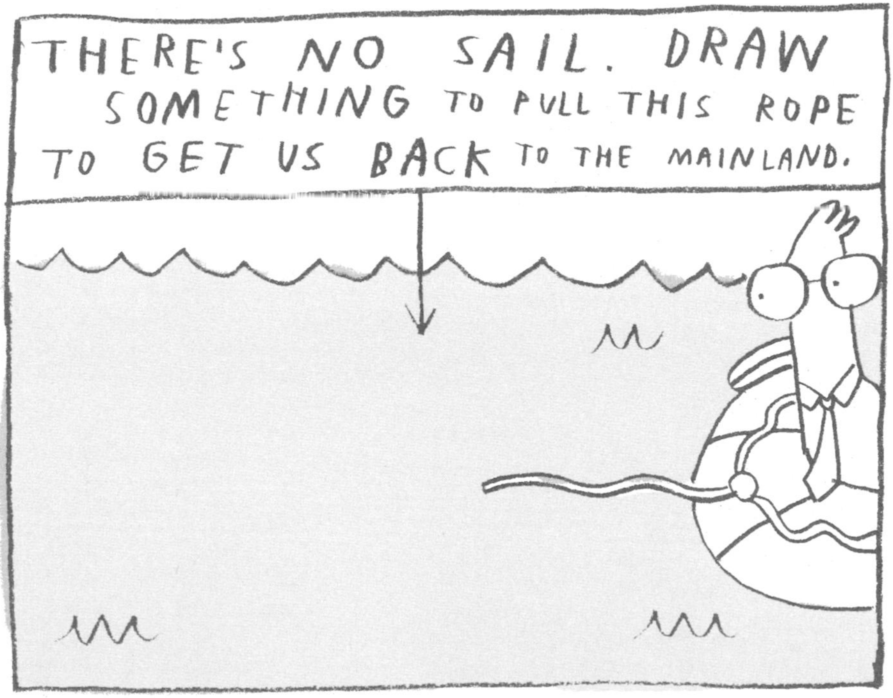
THERE'S NO SAIL. DRAW SOMETHING TO PULL THIS ROPE TO GET US BACK TO THE MAINLAND.

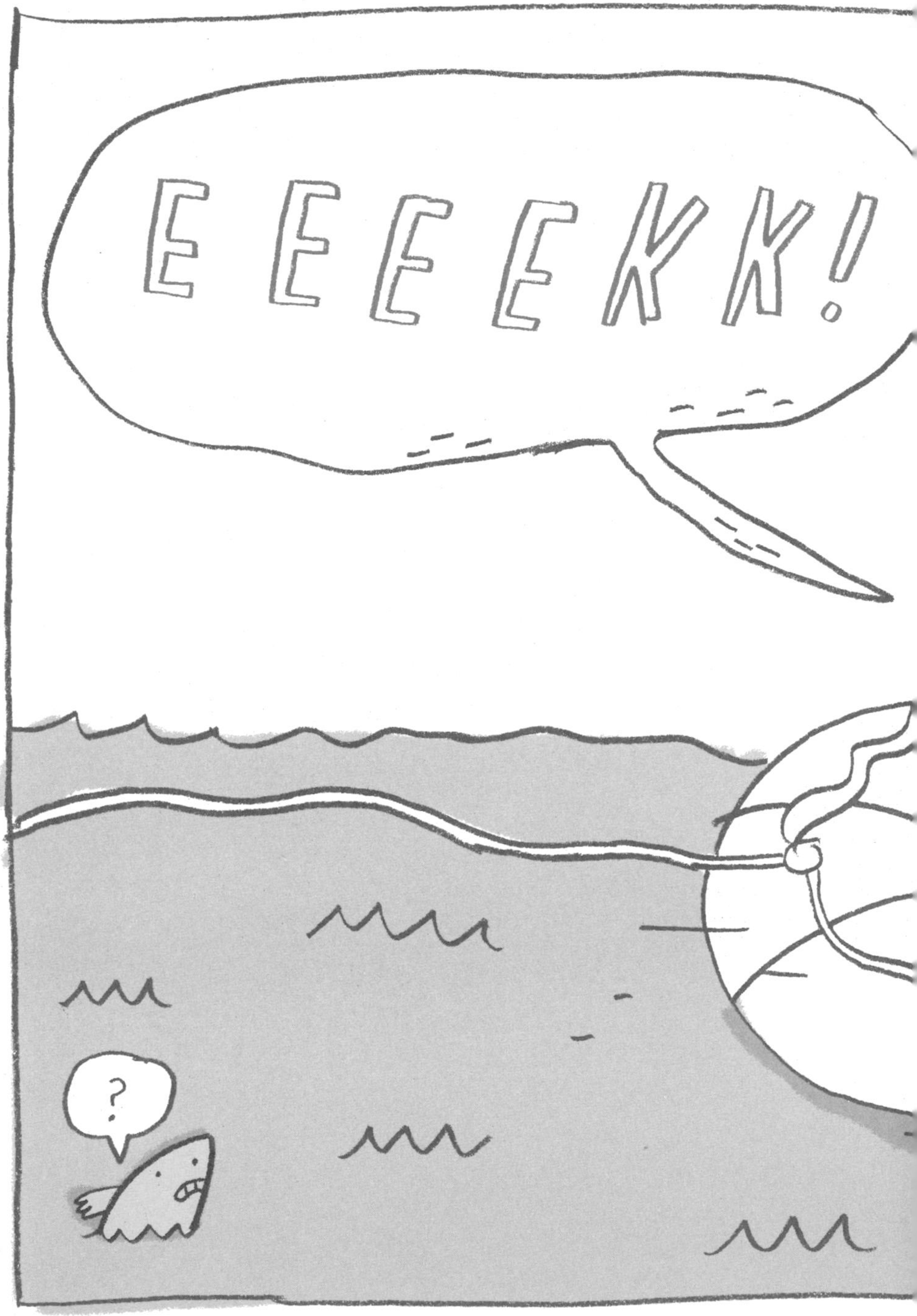
EEEEKK!
?

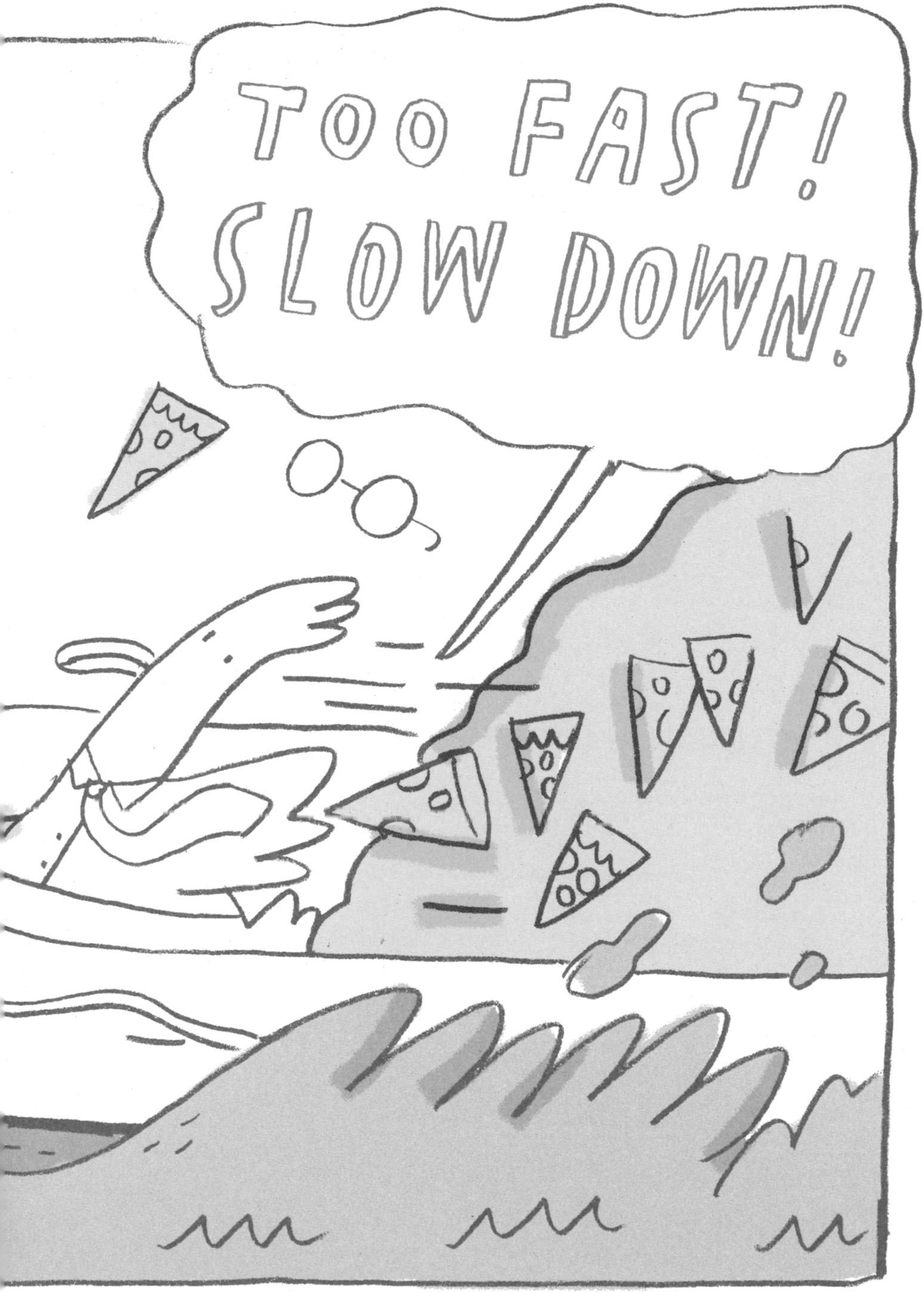
TOO FAST! SLOW DOWN!

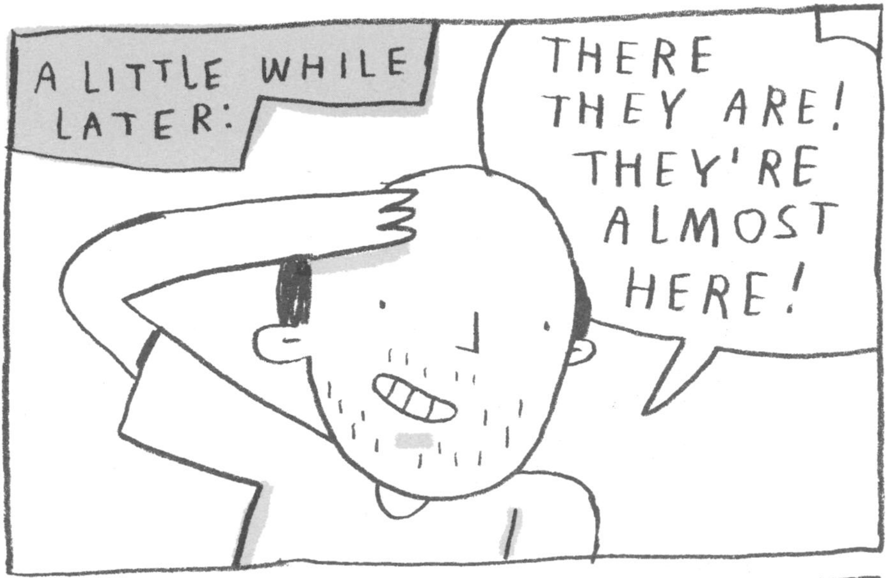
A LITTLE WHILE LATER:
THERE THEY ARE! THEY'RE ALMOST HERE!

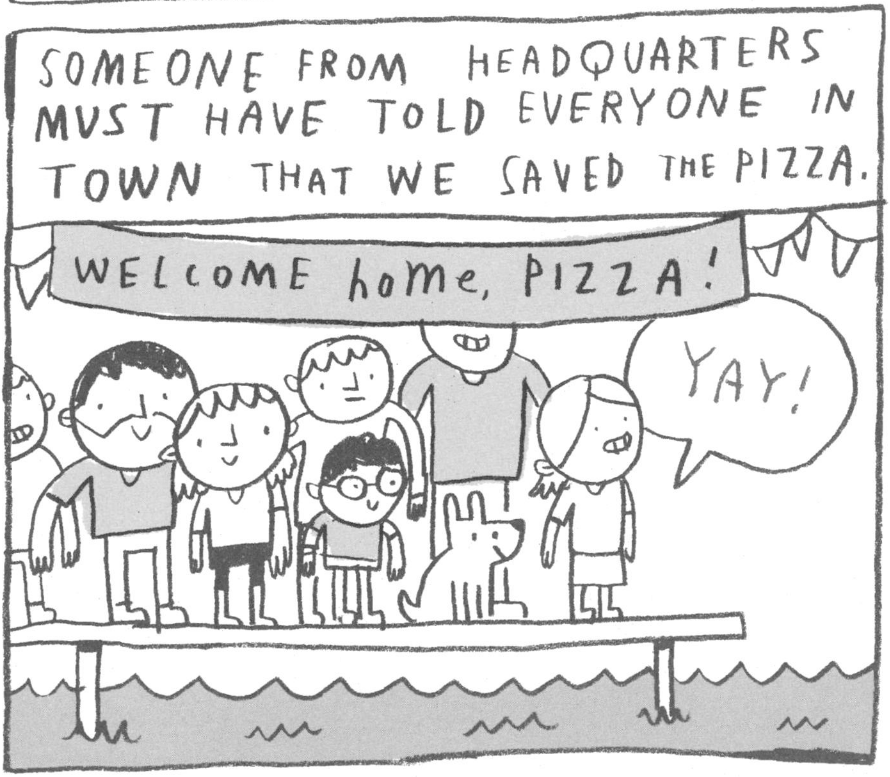
SOMEONE FROM HEADQUARTERS MUST HAVE TOLD EVERYONE IN TOWN THAT WE SAVED THE PIZZA.
WELCOME home, PIZZA!
YAY!

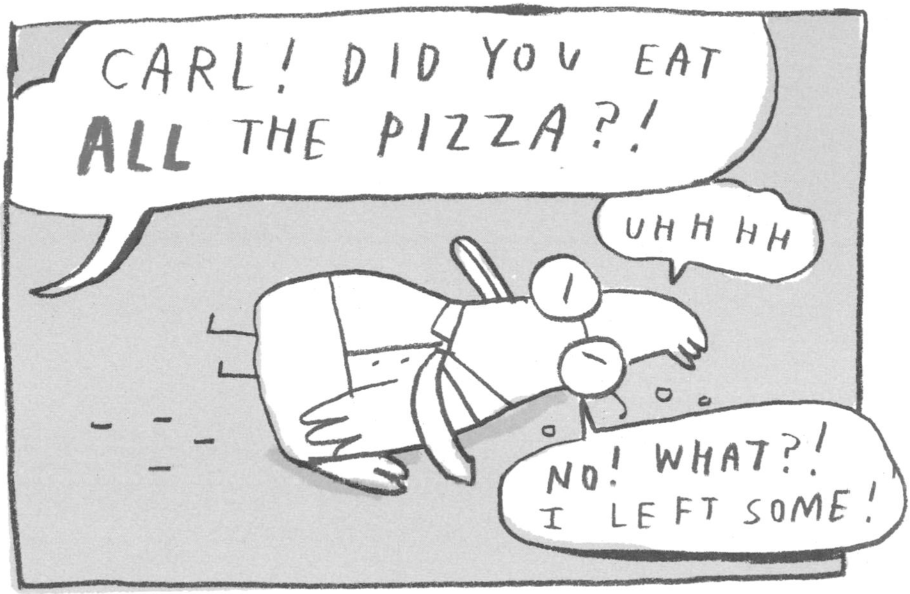
CARL! DID YOU EAT **ALL** THE PIZZA?!
UHHHH
NO! WHAT?! I LEFT SOME!

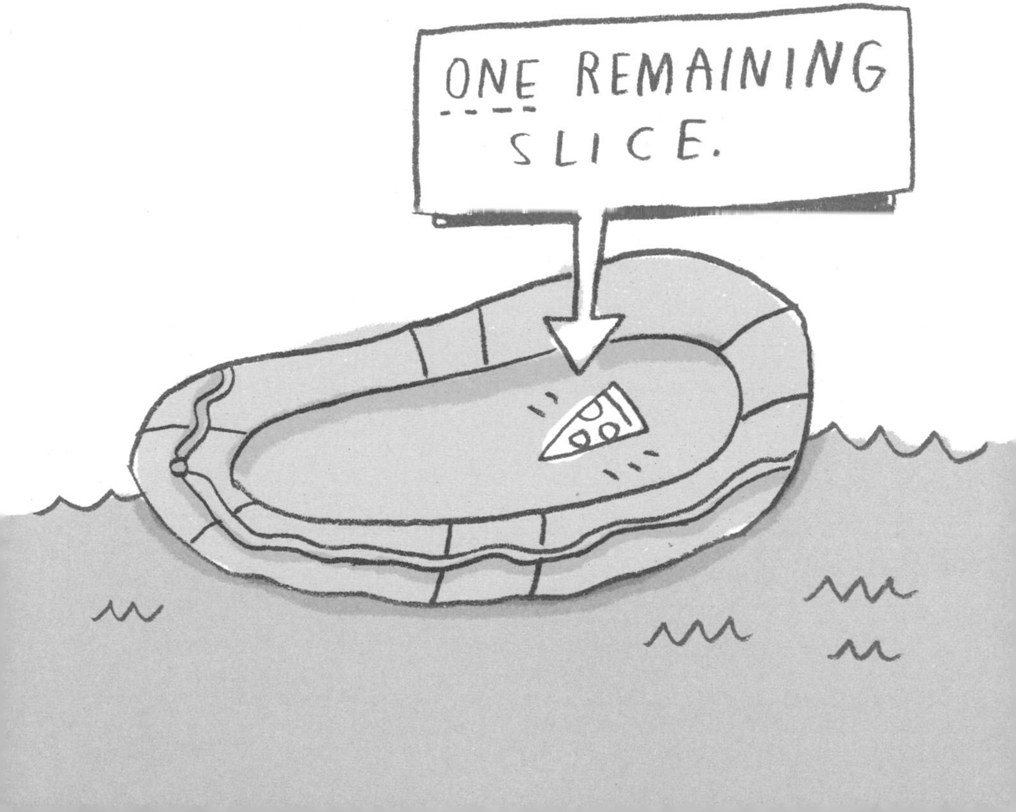
ONE REMAINING SLICE.

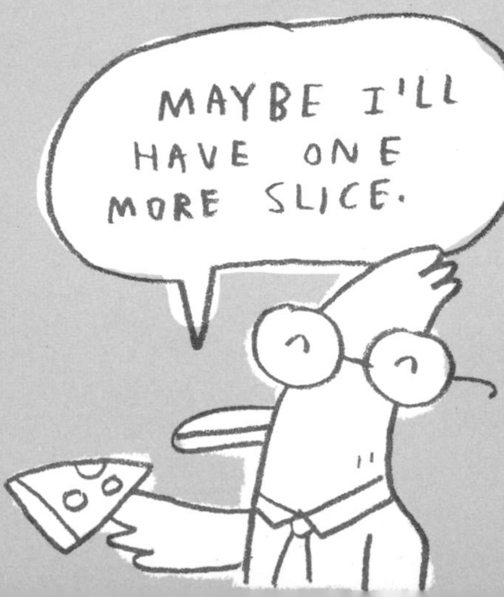
MAYBE I'LL HAVE ONE MORE SLICE.

THE
END

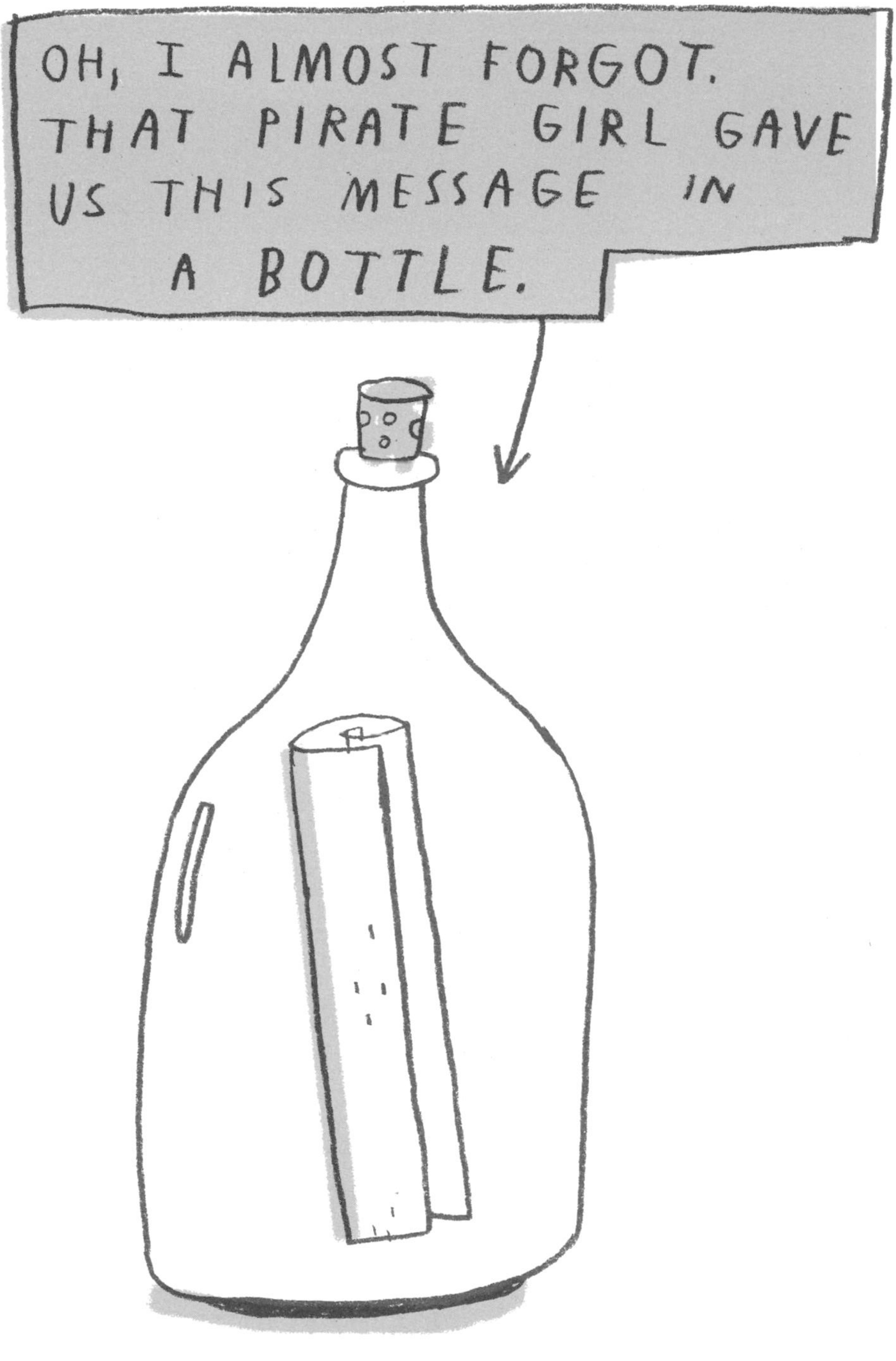
OH, I ALMOST FORGOT. THAT PIRATE GIRL GAVE US THIS MESSAGE IN A BOTTLE.